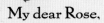

My dear Rose,

Our stay on the planet of Jade was an eye-opener for me.
I finally understand how Fox feels and how he looks at our
friendship.

I've always thought of him as my closest friend. That was
obvious enough to me. However, just thinking things isn't
enough. It's important to let others know what they mean to
us. I've also discovered that Fox underestimates his role in
our pursuit of the Snake. But thanks to Jade and her sons,
we're on the same wavelength from now on. At least, I think
so! You know how Fox is!

I hope that my letters let you know how much I miss you.
I'm going to have to sign off now, because our plane is caught
in an interstellar storm and there's hardly any light here
anymore, as if the stars were all destroyed in this sector...
Could it be the Snake's doing?

The Little Prince

First American edition published in 2013 by Graphic Universe™.

Le Petit Prince ™

based on the masterpiece by Antoine de Saint-Exupéry

© 2013 LPPM
An animated series based on the novel *Le Petit Prince* by Antoine de Saint-Exupéry
Developed for television by Matthieu Delaporte, Alexandre de la Patellière, and Bertrand Gatignol
Directed by Pierre-Alain Chartier

© 2013 ÉDITIONS GLÉNAT
Copyright © 2013 by Lerner Publishing Group, Inc., for the current edition

Graphic Universe™
A division of Lerner Publishing Group, Inc.
241 First Avenue North
Minneapolis, MN 55401 U.S.A.

Website address: www.lernerbooks.com

Library of Congress Cataloging-in-Publication Data

Barichella, Thomas.
    [Planète de l'astronome. English]
    The star snatcher's planet / story by Thomas Barichella ; design and illustrations by Élyum Studio ; adaptation by Guillaume Dorison ; translation, Carol Klio Burrell. — 1st American ed.
        p.   cm. — (The little prince ; #05)
    ISBN 978-0-7613-8755-8 (lib. bdg. : alk. paper)
    1. Graphic novels. I. Dorison, Guillaume. II. Burrell, Carol Klio. III. Saint-Exupéry, Antoine de, 1900-1944. Petit prince. IV. Élyum Studio. V. Petit Prince (Television program) VI. Title.
PZ7.7.B356Pl 2013
741.5'944—dc23   2012028620

Manufactured in the United States of America
1 — DP — 12/31/12

THE NEW ADVENTURES
BASED ON THE MASTERPIECE BY ANTOINE DE SAINT-EXUPÉRY

The Little Prince

THE STAR SNATCHER'S PLANET

Based on the animated series and an original story by Thomas Barichella

Design: Élyum Studio
Story: Guillaume Dorison
Artistic Direction: Didier Poli
Art: Diane Fayolle
Backgrounds: Jérôme Benoit
Coloring: Paul Drouin
Editing: Didier Poli
Editorial Consultant: Didier Convard

Translation: Carol Burrell
Bonus Story Translation: Anne and Owen Smith

Graphic Universe™ • Minneapolis • New York

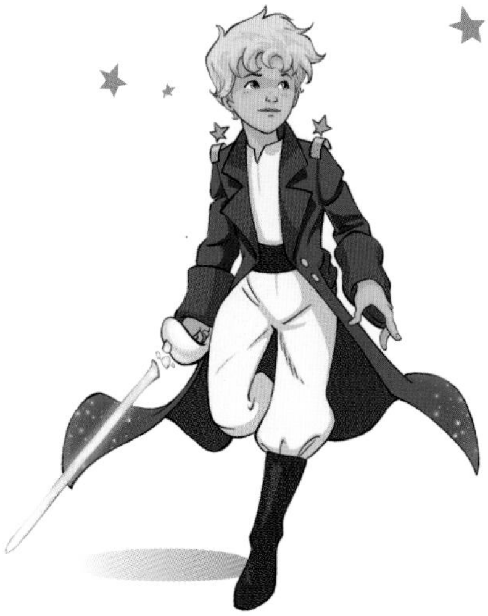

★ THE LITTLE PRINCE

The Little Prince has extraordinary gifts. His sense of wonder allows him to discover what no one else can see. The Little Prince can communicate with all the beings in the universe, even the animals and plants. His powers grow over the course of his adventures.

The Prince's uniform:
When he transforms into the uniform of a prince, he is more agile and quick. When faced with difficult situations, the Little Prince also uses a sword that lets him sketch and bring to life anything from his imagination.

His sketchbook:
When he is not in his Prince's clothing, the Little Prince carries a sketchbook. When he blows on the pages, they take wing and form objects that he'll find very useful. Like his sword, it's powered by stardust collected on his travels.

★ FOX

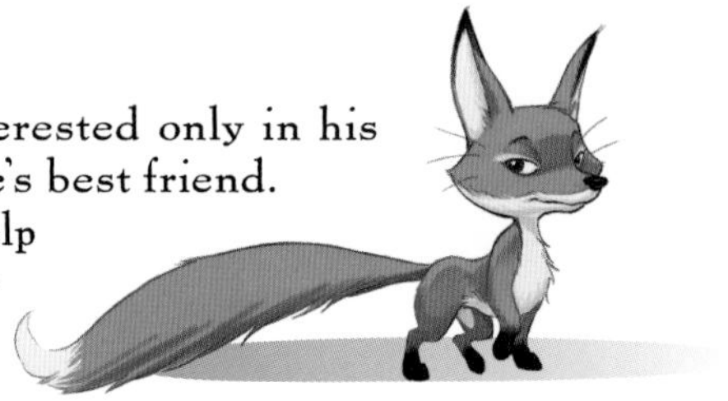

A grouch, a trickster, and, so he says, interested only in his next meal, Fox is in reality the Little Prince's best friend. As such, he is always there to give him help but also just as much to help him to grow and to learn about the world.

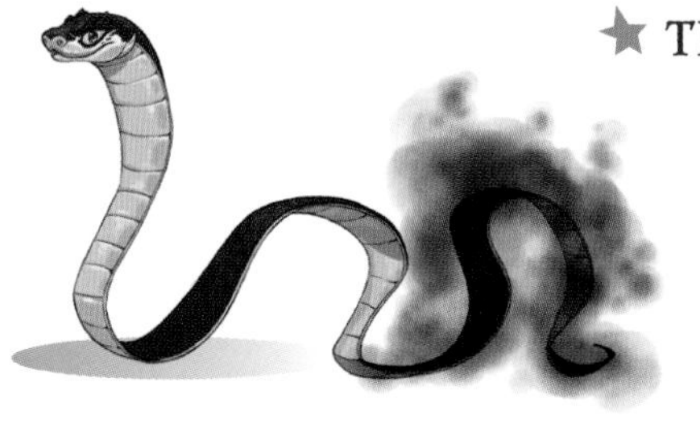

★ THE SNAKE

Even though the Little Prince still does not know exactly why, there can be no doubt that the Snake has set his mind to plunging the entire universe into darkness! And to accomplish his goal, this malicious being is ready to use any form of deception. However, the Snake never takes action himself. He prefers to bring out the wickedness in those beings he has chosen to bite, tempting them to put their own worlds in danger.

★ THE GLOOMIES

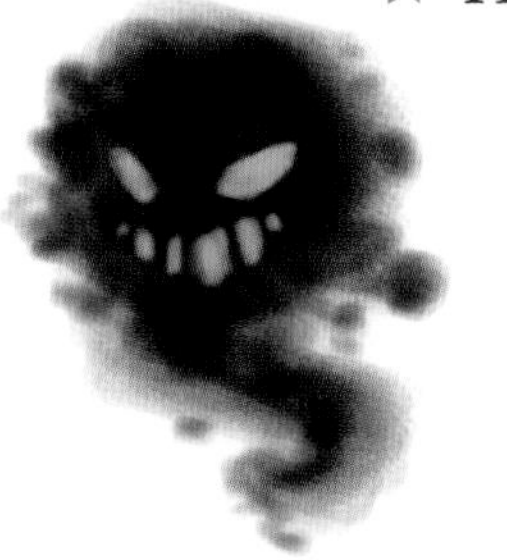

When people who have been "bitten" by the Snake have completely destroyed their own planets, they become Gloomies, slaves to their Snake master. The Gloomies act as a group and carry out the Snake's most vile orders so he can get the better of the Little Prince!

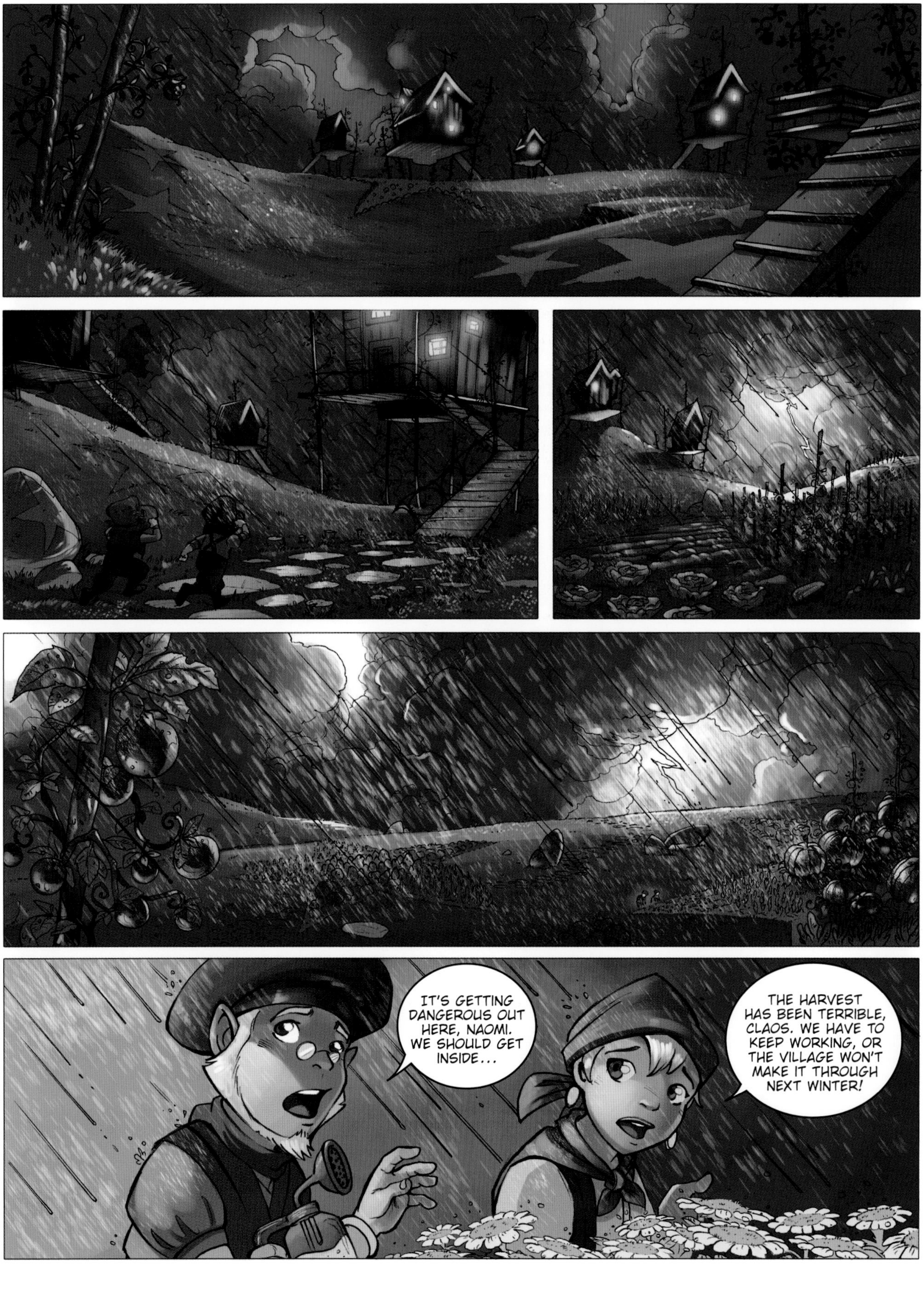
IT'S GETTING DANGEROUS OUT HERE, NAOMI. WE SHOULD GET INSIDE...
THE HARVEST HAS BEEN TERRIBLE, CLAOS. WE HAVE TO KEEP WORKING, OR THE VILLAGE WON'T MAKE IT THROUGH NEXT WINTER!

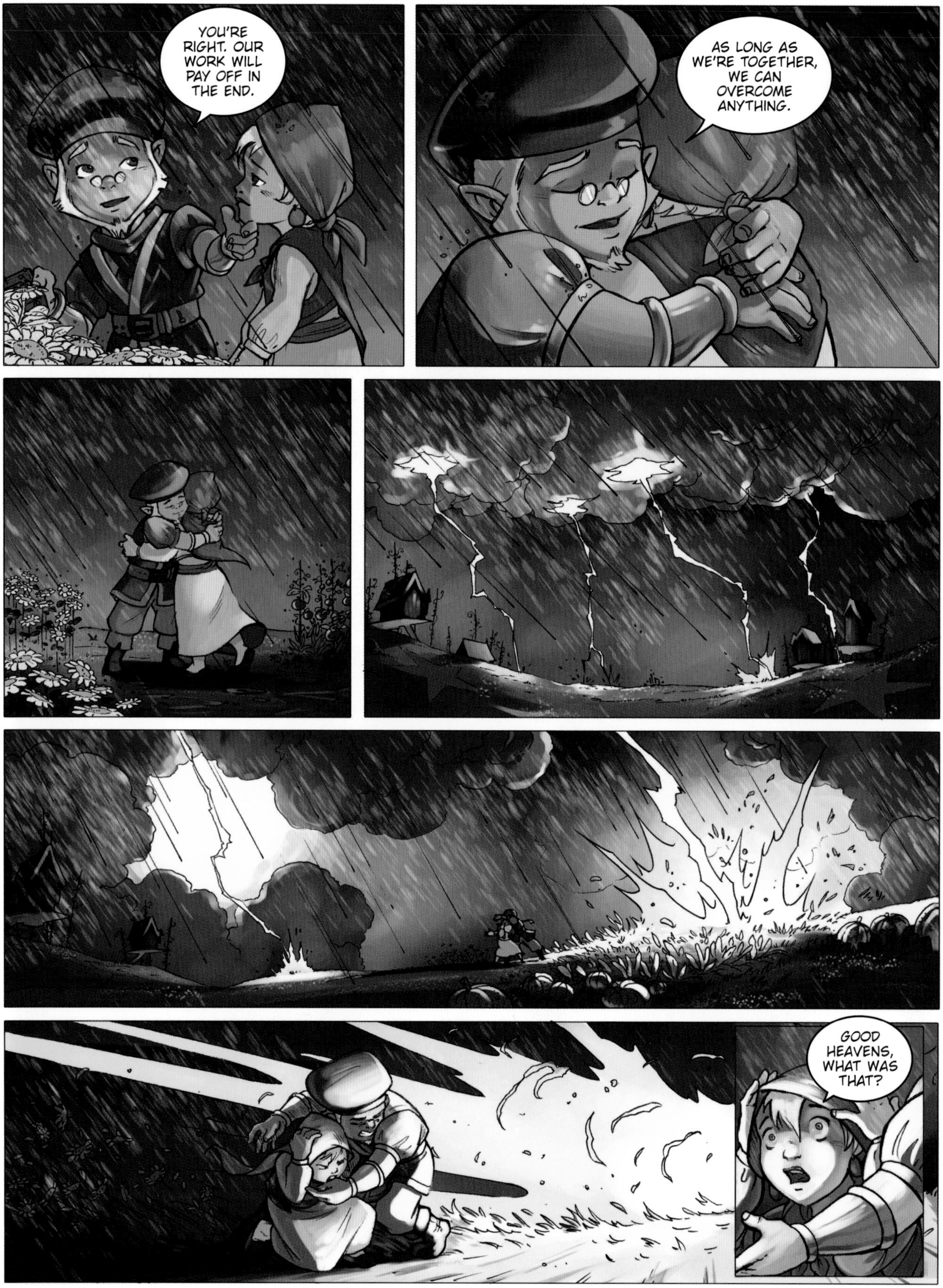
YOU'RE RIGHT. OUR WORK WILL PAY OFF IN THE END.
AS LONG AS WE'RE TOGETHER, WE CAN OVERCOME ANYTHING.
GOOD HEAVENS, WHAT WAS THAT?

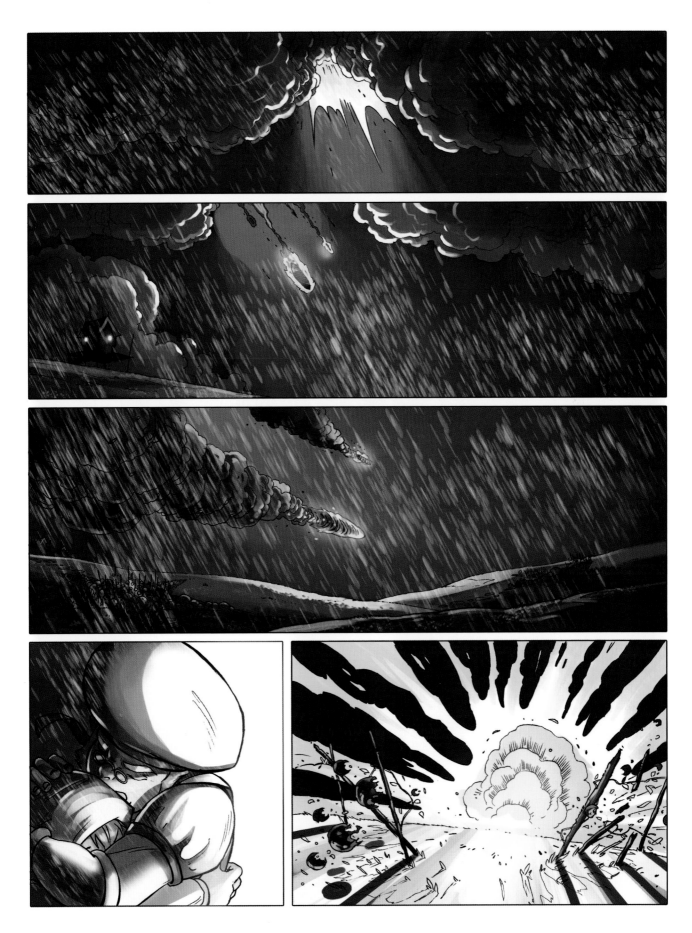

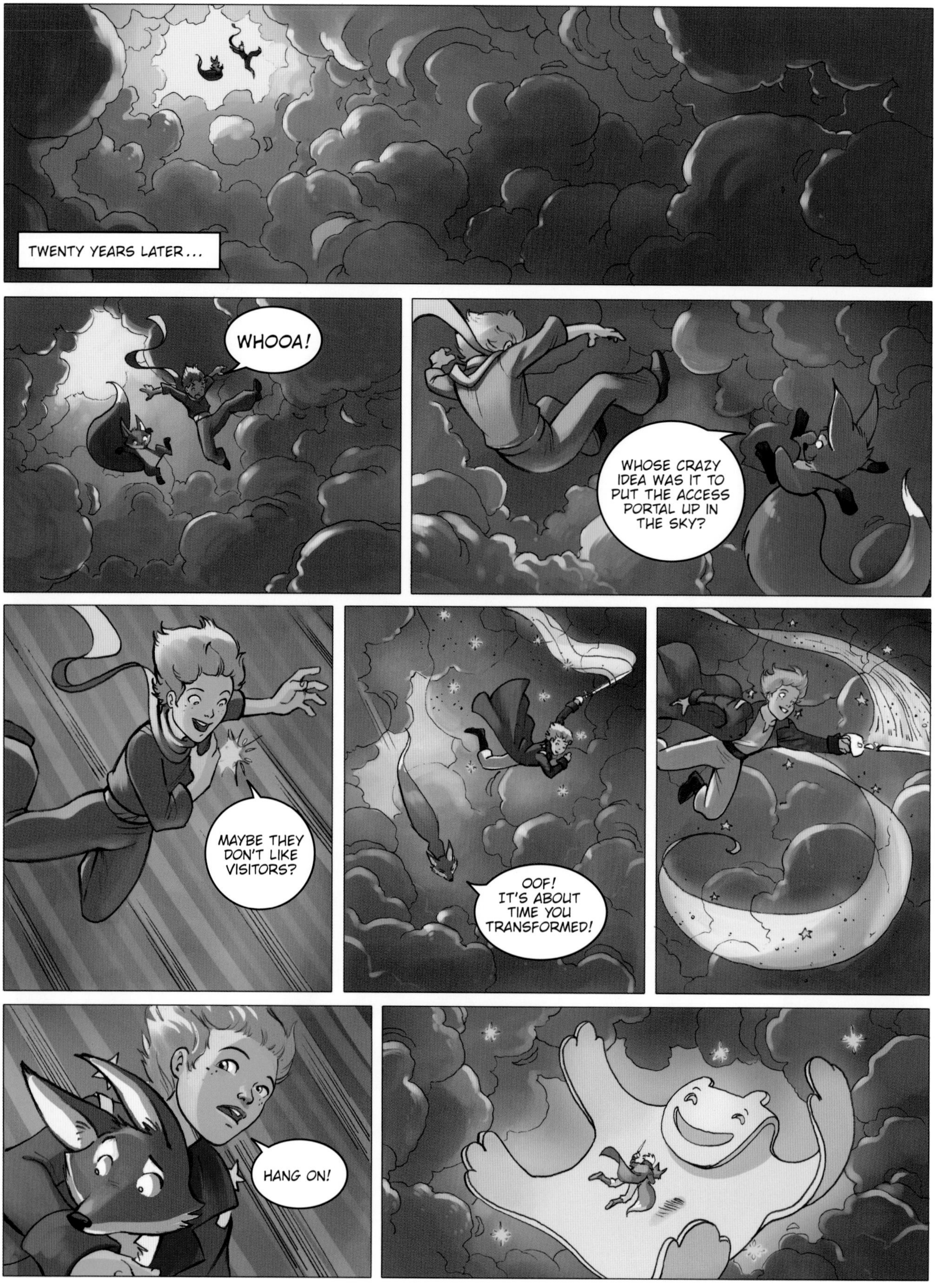

TWENTY YEARS LATER...
WHOOA!
WHOSE CRAZY IDEA WAS IT TO PUT THE ACCESS PORTAL UP IN THE SKY?
MAYBE THEY DON'T LIKE VISITORS?
OOF! IT'S ABOUT TIME YOU TRANSFORMED!
HANG ON!

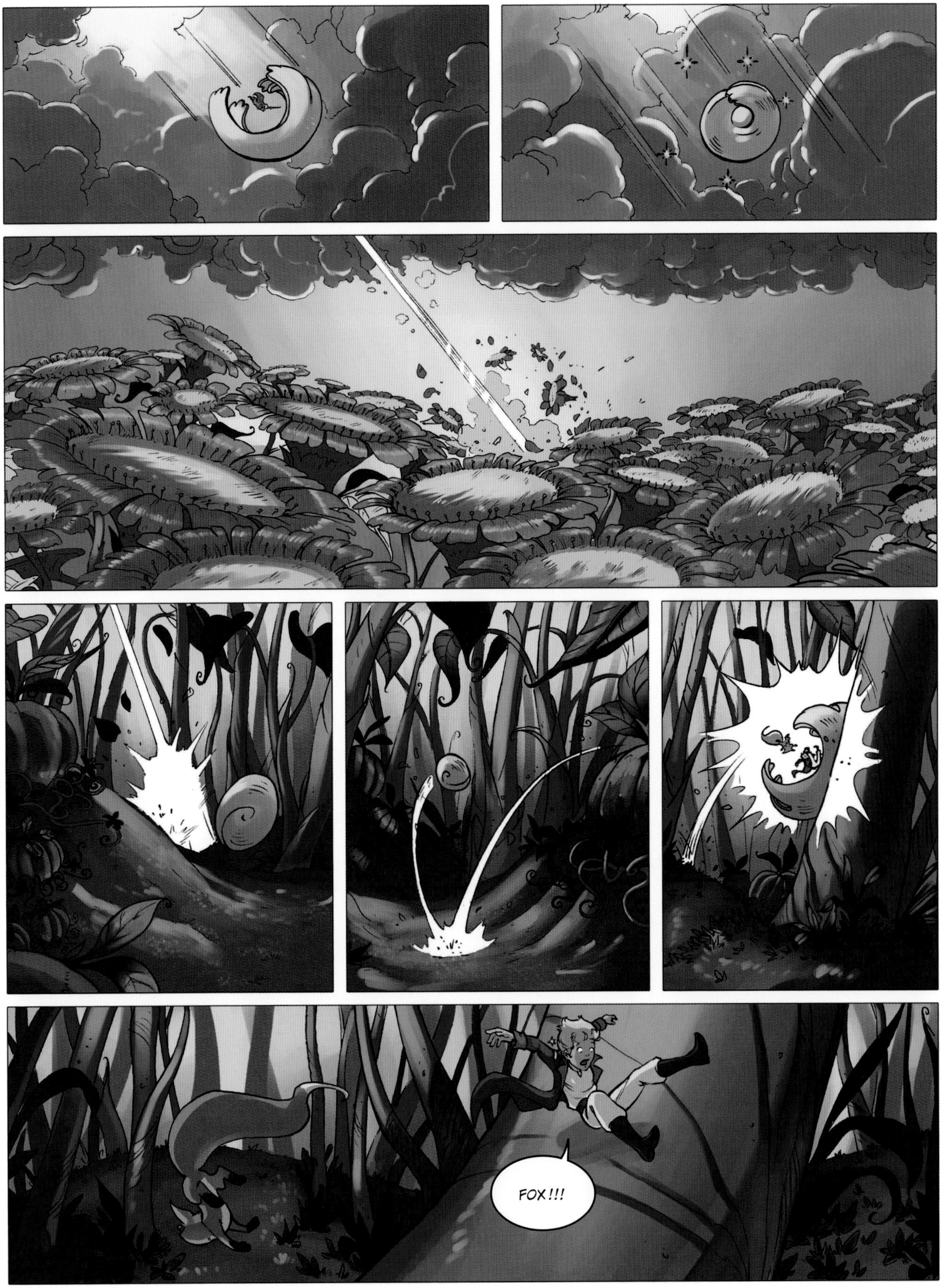
FOX!!!

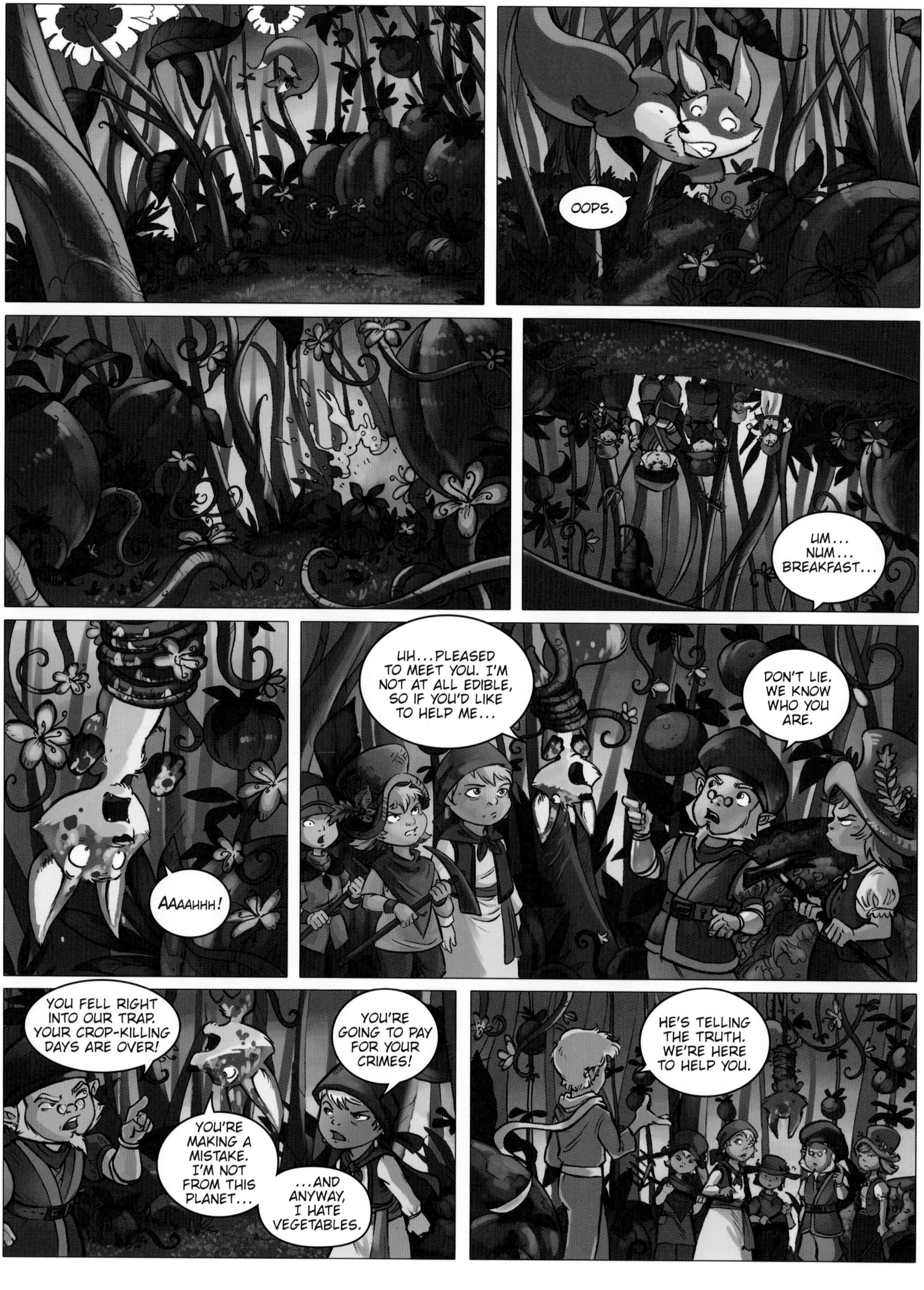
OOPS.
UM... NUM... BREAKFAST...
AAAAHHH!
UH...PLEASED TO MEET YOU. I'M NOT AT ALL EDIBLE, SO IF YOU'D LIKE TO HELP ME...
DON'T LIE. WE KNOW WHO YOU ARE.
YOU FELL RIGHT INTO OUR TRAP. YOUR CROP-KILLING DAYS ARE OVER!
YOU'RE GOING TO PAY FOR YOUR CRIMES!
YOU'RE MAKING A MISTAKE. I'M NOT FROM THIS PLANET...
...AND ANYWAY, I HATE VEGETABLES.
HE'S TELLING THE TRUTH. WE'RE HERE TO HELP YOU.

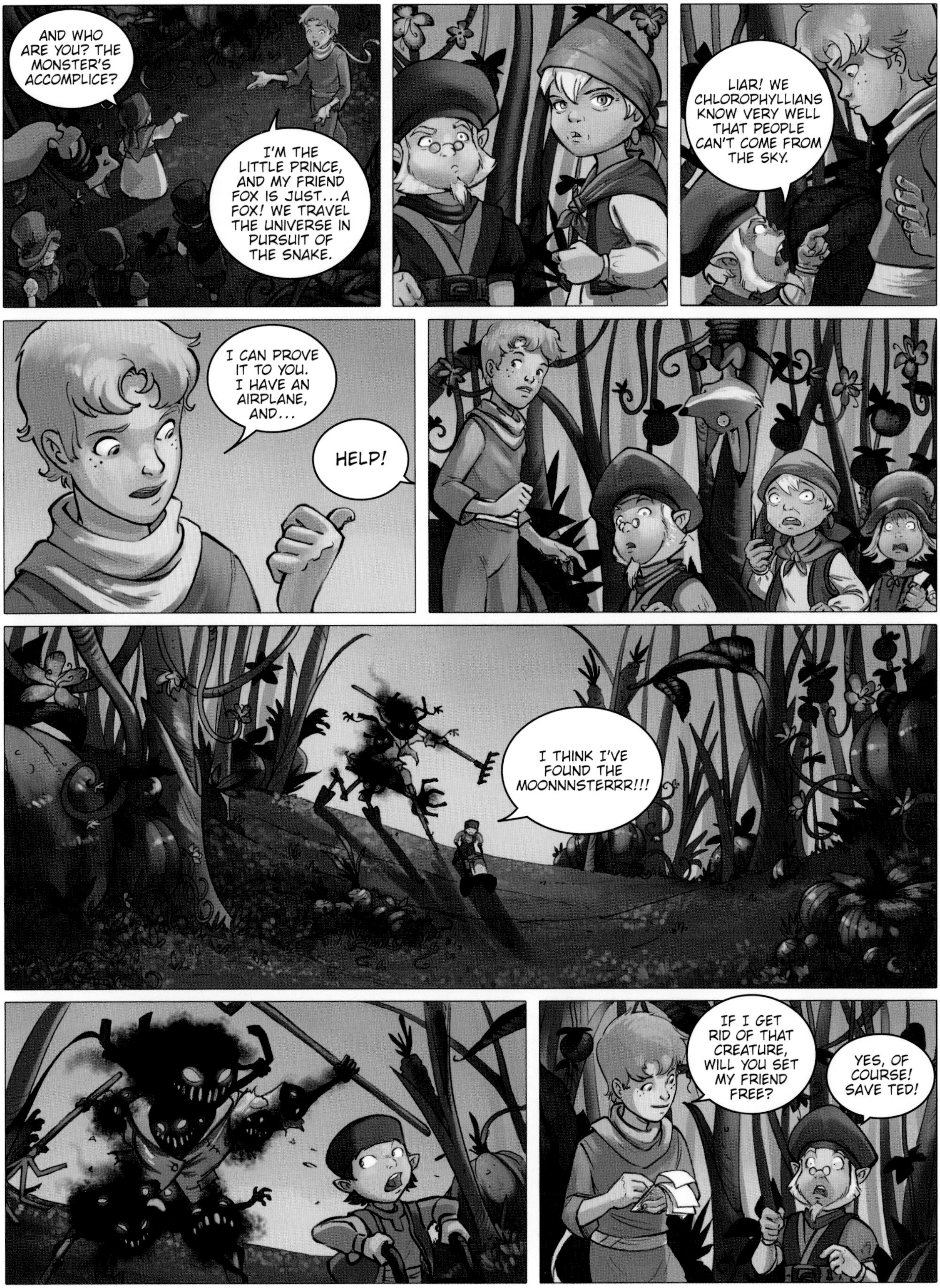
AND WHO ARE YOU? THE MONSTER'S ACCOMPLICE?
I'M THE LITTLE PRINCE, AND MY FRIEND FOX IS JUST...A FOX! WE TRAVEL THE UNIVERSE IN PURSUIT OF THE SNAKE.
LIAR! WE CHLOROPHYLLIANS KNOW VERY WELL THAT PEOPLE CAN'T COME FROM THE SKY.
I CAN PROVE IT TO YOU. I HAVE AN AIRPLANE, AND...
HELP!
I THINK I'VE FOUND THE MOONNNSTERRR!!!
IF I GET RID OF THAT CREATURE, WILL YOU SET MY FRIEND FREE?
YES, OF COURSE! SAVE TED!

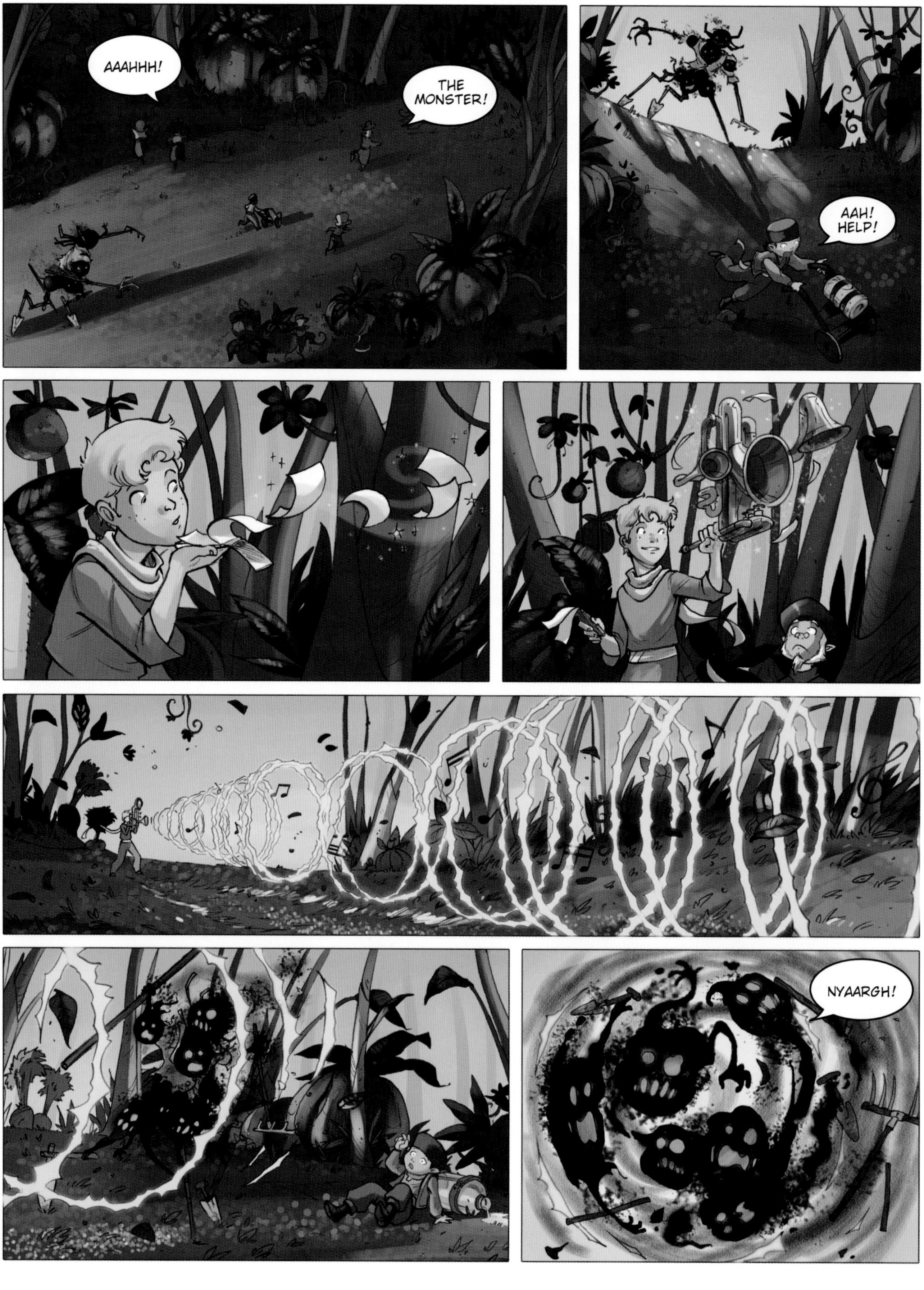
AAAHHH!
THE MONSTER!
AAH! HELP!
NYAARGH!

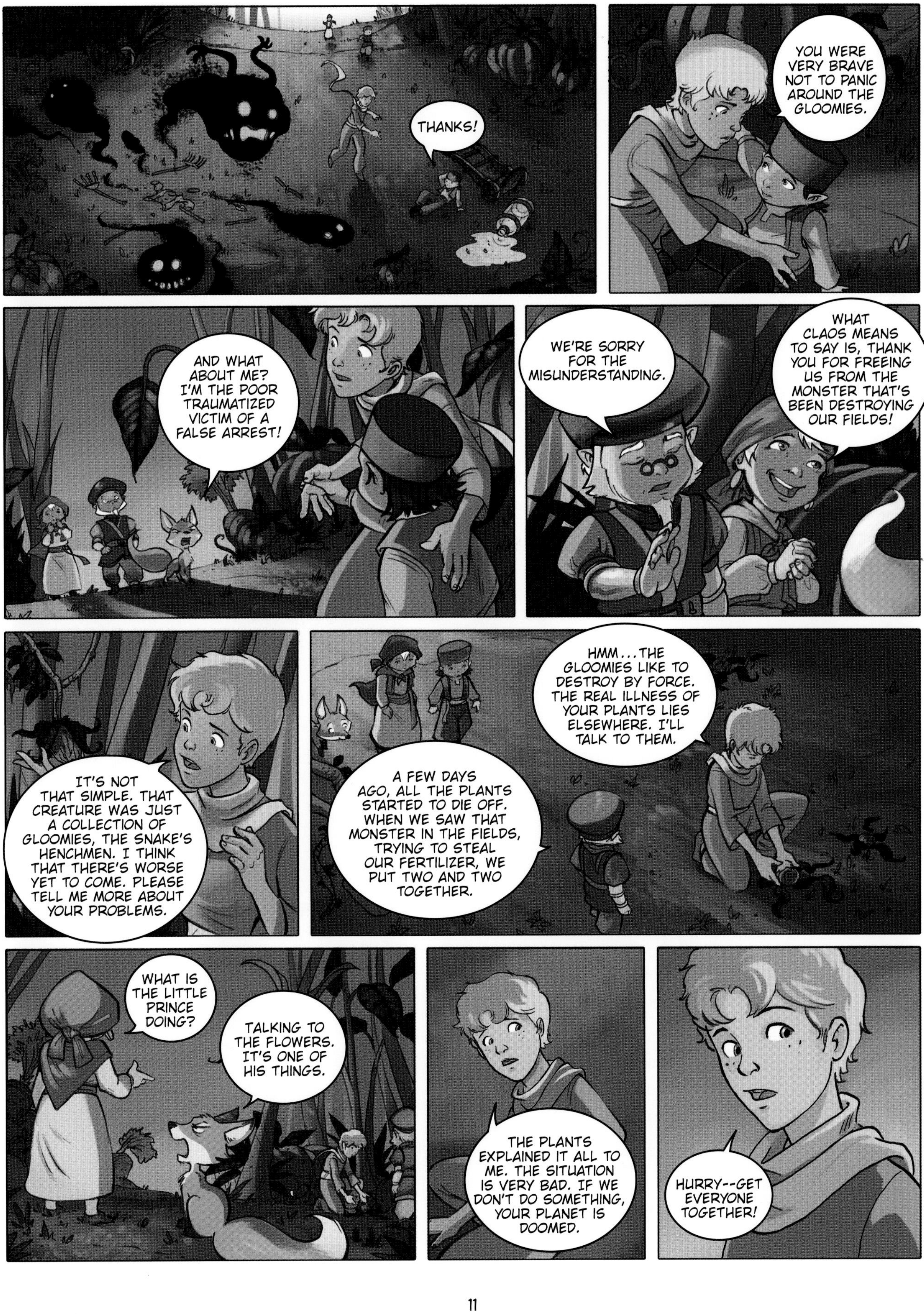
THANKS!
YOU WERE VERY BRAVE NOT TO PANIC AROUND THE GLOOMIES.
AND WHAT ABOUT ME? I'M THE POOR TRAUMATIZED VICTIM OF A FALSE ARREST!
WE'RE SORRY FOR THE MISUNDERSTANDING.
WHAT CLAOS MEANS TO SAY IS, THANK YOU FOR FREEING US FROM THE MONSTER THAT'S BEEN DESTROYING OUR FIELDS!
IT'S NOT THAT SIMPLE. THAT CREATURE WAS JUST A COLLECTION OF GLOOMIES, THE SNAKE'S HENCHMEN. I THINK THAT THERE'S WORSE YET TO COME. PLEASE TELL ME MORE ABOUT YOUR PROBLEMS.
A FEW DAYS AGO, ALL THE PLANTS STARTED TO DIE OFF. WHEN WE SAW THAT MONSTER IN THE FIELDS, TRYING TO STEAL OUR FERTILIZER, WE PUT TWO AND TWO TOGETHER.
HMM... THE GLOOMIES LIKE TO DESTROY BY FORCE. THE REAL ILLNESS OF YOUR PLANTS LIES ELSEWHERE. I'LL TALK TO THEM.
WHAT IS THE LITTLE PRINCE DOING?
TALKING TO THE FLOWERS. IT'S ONE OF HIS THINGS.
THE PLANTS EXPLAINED IT ALL TO ME. THE SITUATION IS VERY BAD. IF WE DON'T DO SOMETHING, YOUR PLANET IS DOOMED.
HURRY--GET EVERYONE TOGETHER!

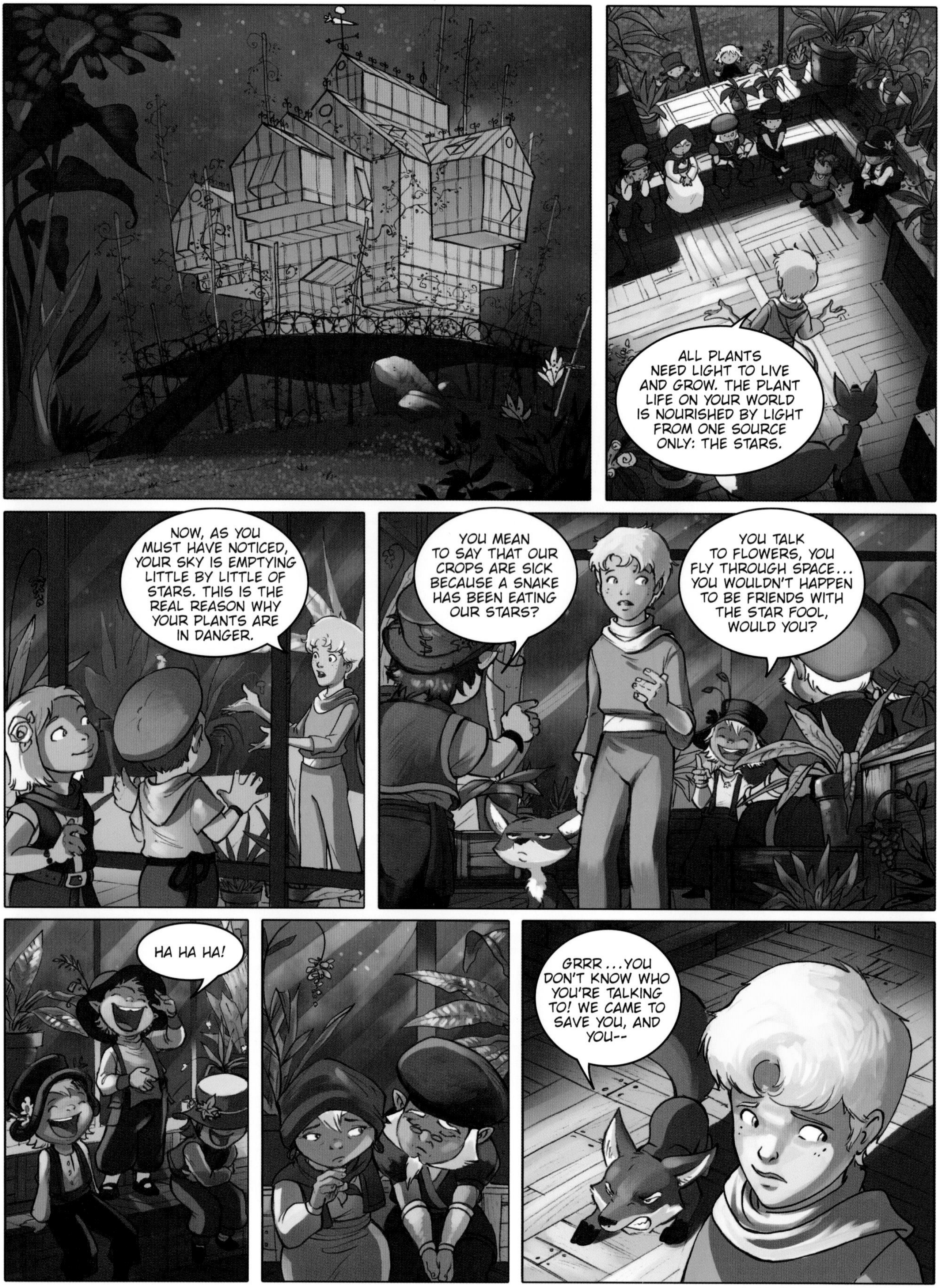
ALL PLANTS NEED LIGHT TO LIVE AND GROW. THE PLANT LIFE ON YOUR WORLD IS NOURISHED BY LIGHT FROM ONE SOURCE ONLY: THE STARS.
NOW, AS YOU MUST HAVE NOTICED, YOUR SKY IS EMPTYING LITTLE BY LITTLE OF STARS. THIS IS THE REAL REASON WHY YOUR PLANTS ARE IN DANGER.
YOU MEAN TO SAY THAT OUR CROPS ARE SICK BECAUSE A SNAKE HAS BEEN EATING OUR STARS?
YOU TALK TO FLOWERS, YOU FLY THROUGH SPACE... YOU WOULDN'T HAPPEN TO BE FRIENDS WITH THE STAR FOOL, WOULD YOU?
HA HA HA!
GRRR... YOU DON'T KNOW WHO YOU'RE TALKING TO! WE CAME TO SAVE YOU, AND YOU--

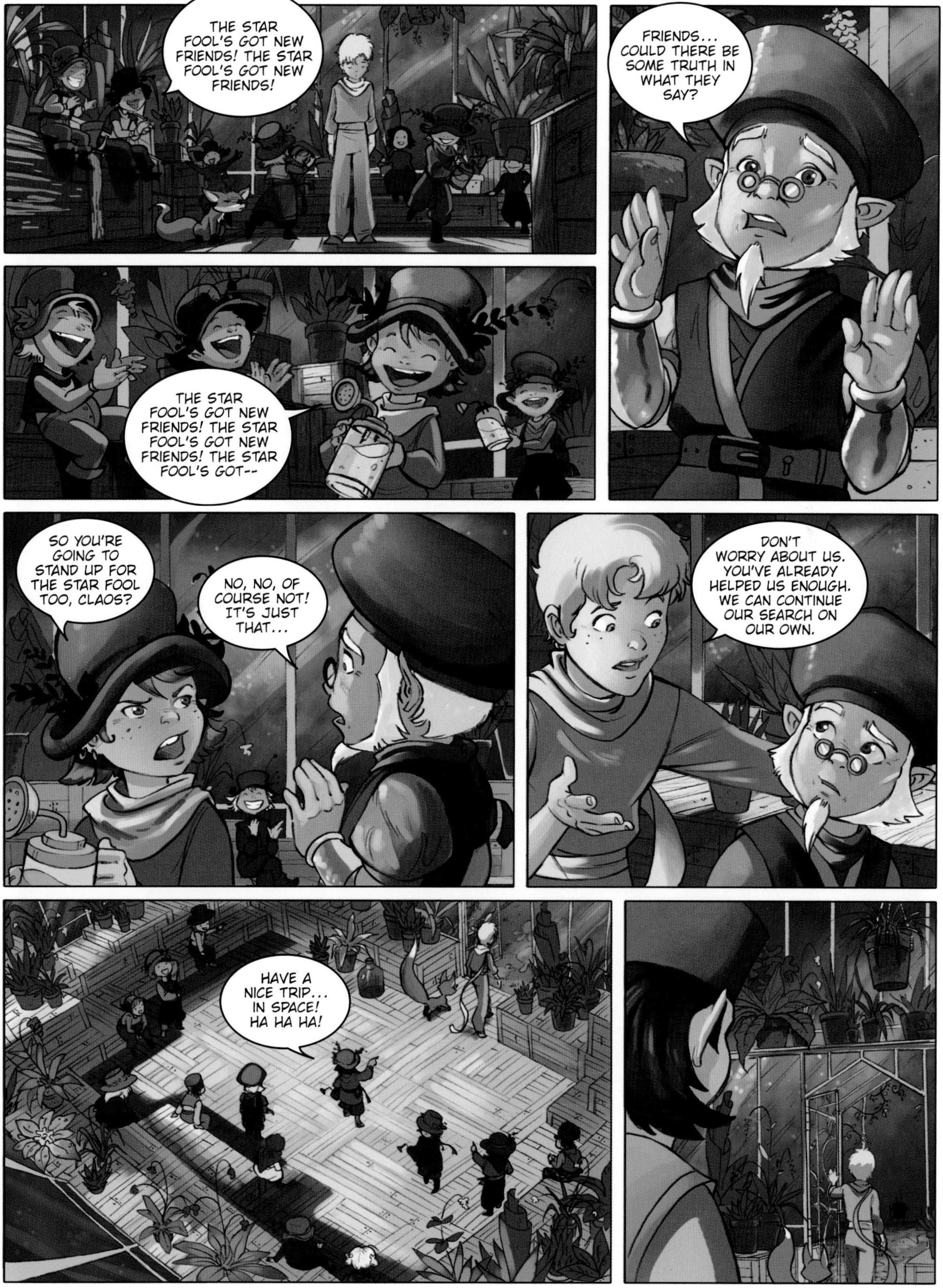
THE STAR FOOL'S GOT NEW FRIENDS! THE STAR FOOL'S GOT NEW FRIENDS!
FRIENDS... COULD THERE BE SOME TRUTH IN WHAT THEY SAY?
THE STAR FOOL'S GOT NEW FRIENDS! THE STAR FOOL'S GOT NEW FRIENDS! THE STAR FOOL'S GOT--
SO YOU'RE GOING TO STAND UP FOR THE STAR FOOL TOO, CLAOS?
NO, NO, OF COURSE NOT! IT'S JUST THAT...
DON'T WORRY ABOUT US. YOU'VE ALREADY HELPED US ENOUGH. WE CAN CONTINUE OUR SEARCH ON OUR OWN.
HAVE A NICE TRIP... IN SPACE! HA HA HA!

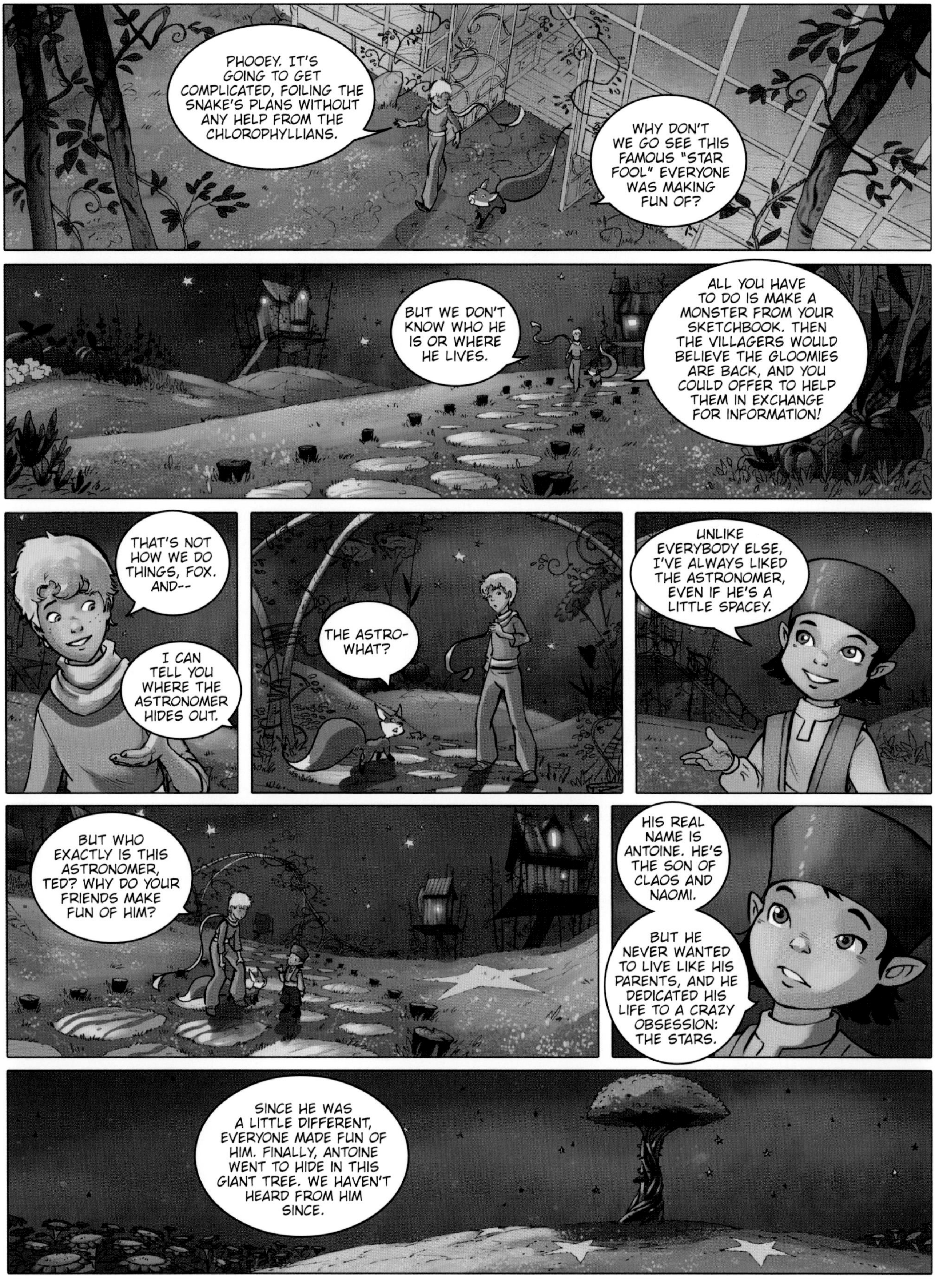

PHOOEY. IT'S GOING TO GET COMPLICATED, FOILING THE SNAKE'S PLANS WITHOUT ANY HELP FROM THE CHLOROPHYLLIANS.
WHY DON'T WE GO SEE THIS FAMOUS "STAR FOOL" EVERYONE WAS MAKING FUN OF?
BUT WE DON'T KNOW WHO HE IS OR WHERE HE LIVES.
ALL YOU HAVE TO DO IS MAKE A MONSTER FROM YOUR SKETCHBOOK. THEN THE VILLAGERS WOULD BELIEVE THE GLOOMIES ARE BACK, AND YOU COULD OFFER TO HELP THEM IN EXCHANGE FOR INFORMATION!
THAT'S NOT HOW WE DO THINGS, FOX. AND--
I CAN TELL YOU WHERE THE ASTRONOMER HIDES OUT.
THE ASTRO-WHAT?
UNLIKE EVERYBODY ELSE, I'VE ALWAYS LIKED THE ASTRONOMER, EVEN IF HE'S A LITTLE SPACEY.
BUT WHO EXACTLY IS THIS ASTRONOMER, TED? WHY DO YOUR FRIENDS MAKE FUN OF HIM?
HIS REAL NAME IS ANTOINE. HE'S THE SON OF CLAOS AND NAOMI.
BUT HE NEVER WANTED TO LIVE LIKE HIS PARENTS, AND HE DEDICATED HIS LIFE TO A CRAZY OBSESSION: THE STARS.
SINCE HE WAS A LITTLE DIFFERENT, EVERYONE MADE FUN OF HIM. FINALLY, ANTOINE WENT TO HIDE IN THIS GIANT TREE. WE HAVEN'T HEARD FROM HIM SINCE.

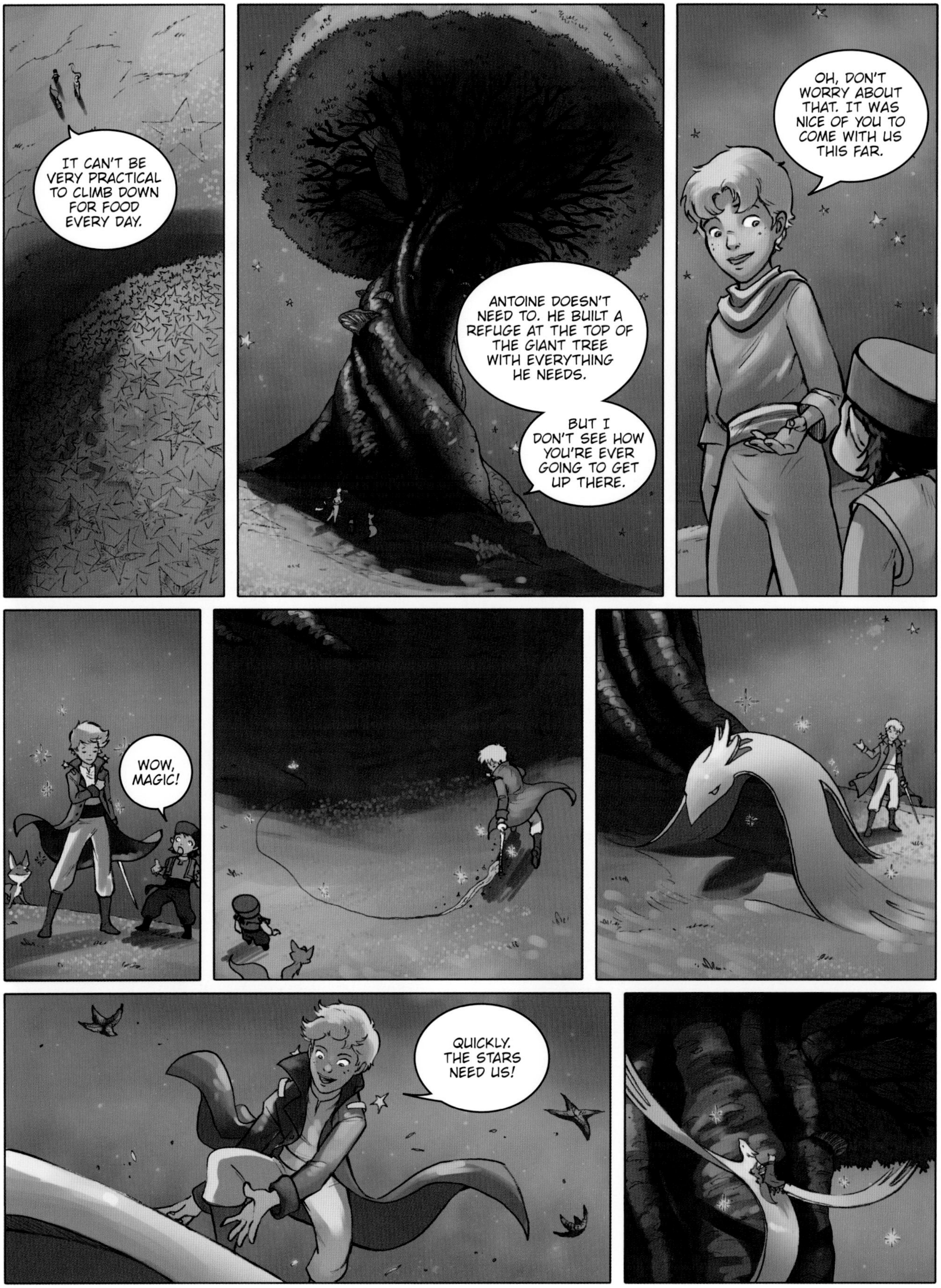
IT CAN'T BE VERY PRACTICAL TO CLIMB DOWN FOR FOOD EVERY DAY.
ANTOINE DOESN'T NEED TO. HE BUILT A REFUGE AT THE TOP OF THE GIANT TREE WITH EVERYTHING HE NEEDS.
BUT I DON'T SEE HOW YOU'RE EVER GOING TO GET UP THERE.
OH, DON'T WORRY ABOUT THAT. IT WAS NICE OF YOU TO COME WITH US THIS FAR.
WOW, MAGIC!
QUICKLY. THE STARS NEED US!

THERE HAS TO BE AN ENTRANCE AROUND HERE SOMEWHERE...

FOUND IT!

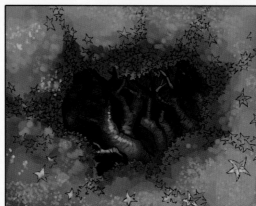

THIS MUST BE IT...

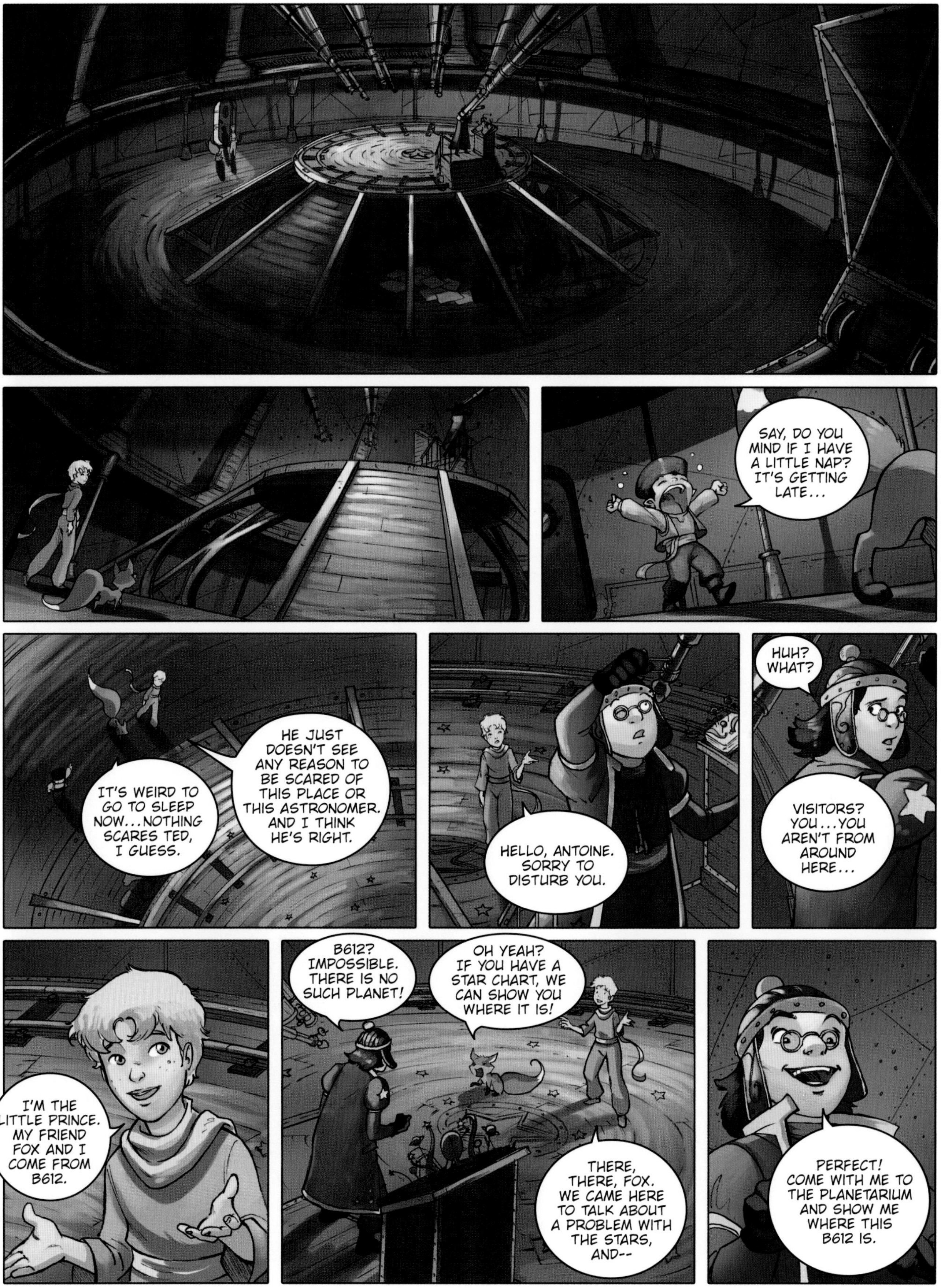

SAY, DO YOU MIND IF I HAVE A LITTLE NAP? IT'S GETTING LATE...
IT'S WEIRD TO GO TO SLEEP NOW...NOTHING SCARES TED, I GUESS.
HE JUST DOESN'T SEE ANY REASON TO BE SCARED OF THIS PLACE OR THIS ASTRONOMER. AND I THINK HE'S RIGHT.
HELLO, ANTOINE. SORRY TO DISTURB YOU.
HUH? WHAT?
VISITORS? YOU...YOU AREN'T FROM AROUND HERE...
I'M THE LITTLE PRINCE. MY FRIEND FOX AND I COME FROM B612.
B612? IMPOSSIBLE. THERE IS NO SUCH PLANET!
OH YEAH? IF YOU HAVE A STAR CHART, WE CAN SHOW YOU WHERE IT IS!
THERE, THERE, FOX. WE CAME HERE TO TALK ABOUT A PROBLEM WITH THE STARS, AND--
PERFECT! COME WITH ME TO THE PLANETARIUM AND SHOW ME WHERE THIS B612 IS.

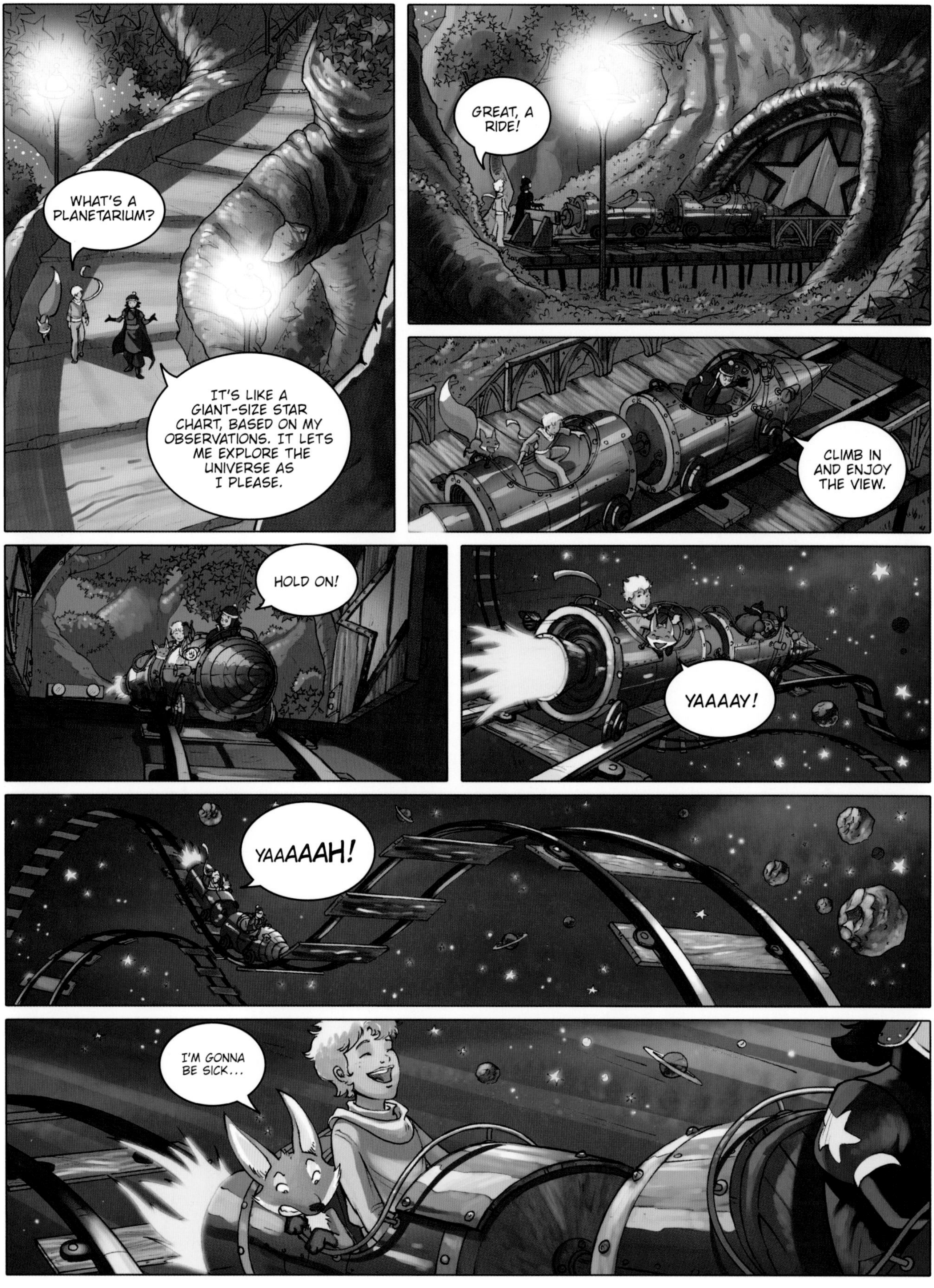
WHAT'S A PLANETARIUM?
IT'S LIKE A GIANT-SIZE STAR CHART, BASED ON MY OBSERVATIONS. IT LETS ME EXPLORE THE UNIVERSE AS I PLEASE.
GREAT, A RIDE!
CLIMB IN AND ENJOY THE VIEW.
HOLD ON!
YAAAAY!
YAAAAAH!
I'M GONNA BE SICK...

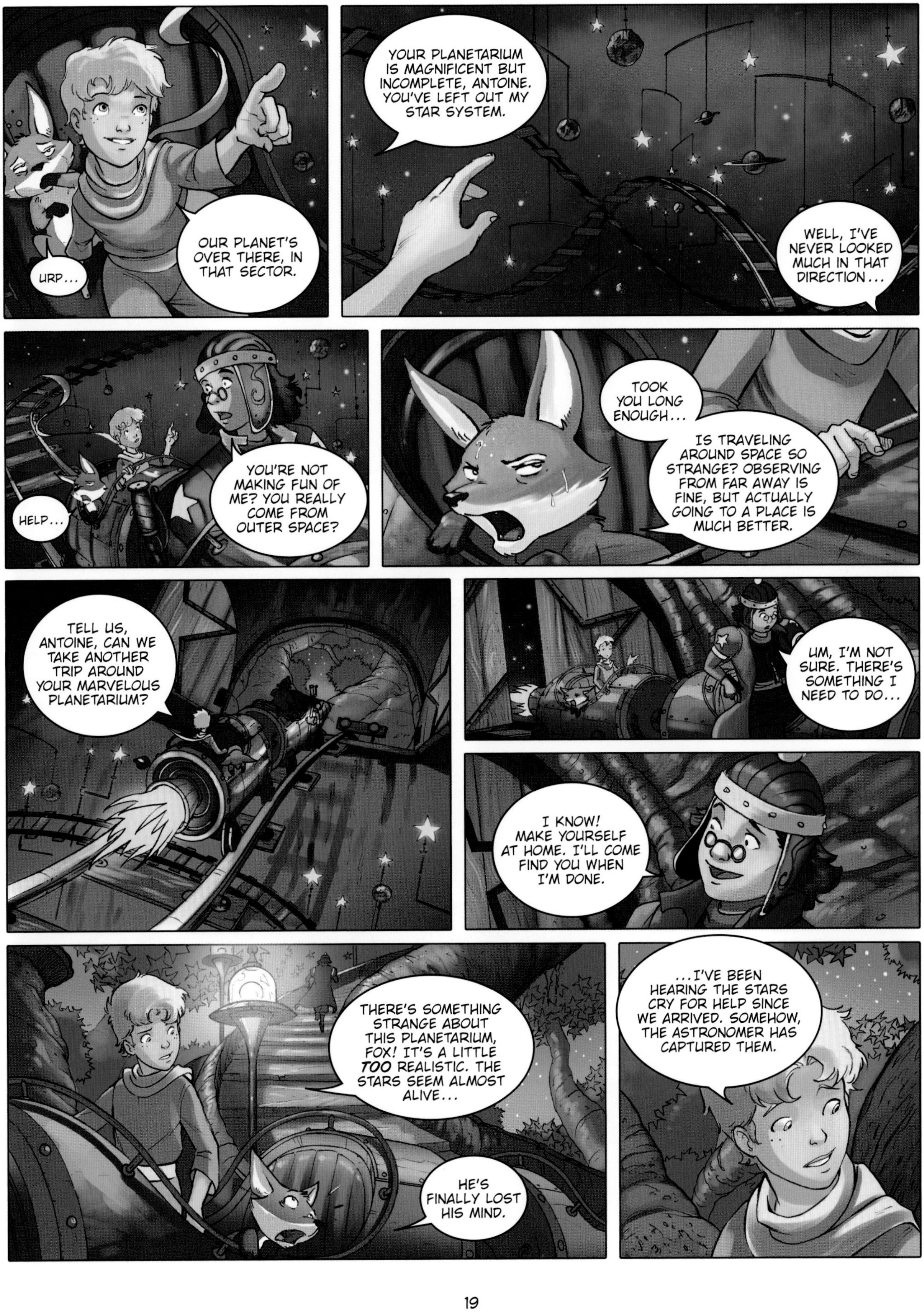
OUR PLANET'S OVER THERE, IN THAT SECTOR.
URP...
YOUR PLANETARIUM IS MAGNIFICENT BUT INCOMPLETE, ANTOINE. YOU'VE LEFT OUT MY STAR SYSTEM.
WELL, I'VE NEVER LOOKED MUCH IN THAT DIRECTION...
YOU'RE NOT MAKING FUN OF ME? YOU REALLY COME FROM OUTER SPACE?
HELP...
TOOK YOU LONG ENOUGH...
IS TRAVELING AROUND SPACE SO STRANGE? OBSERVING FROM FAR AWAY IS FINE, BUT ACTUALLY GOING TO A PLACE IS MUCH BETTER.
TELL US, ANTOINE, CAN WE TAKE ANOTHER TRIP AROUND YOUR MARVELOUS PLANETARIUM?
UM, I'M NOT SURE. THERE'S SOMETHING I NEED TO DO...
I KNOW! MAKE YOURSELF AT HOME. I'LL COME FIND YOU WHEN I'M DONE.
THERE'S SOMETHING STRANGE ABOUT THIS PLANETARIUM, FOX! IT'S A LITTLE TOO REALISTIC. THE STARS SEEM ALMOST ALIVE...
HE'S FINALLY LOST HIS MIND.
...I'VE BEEN HEARING THE STARS CRY FOR HELP SINCE WE ARRIVED. SOMEHOW, THE ASTRONOMER HAS CAPTURED THEM.

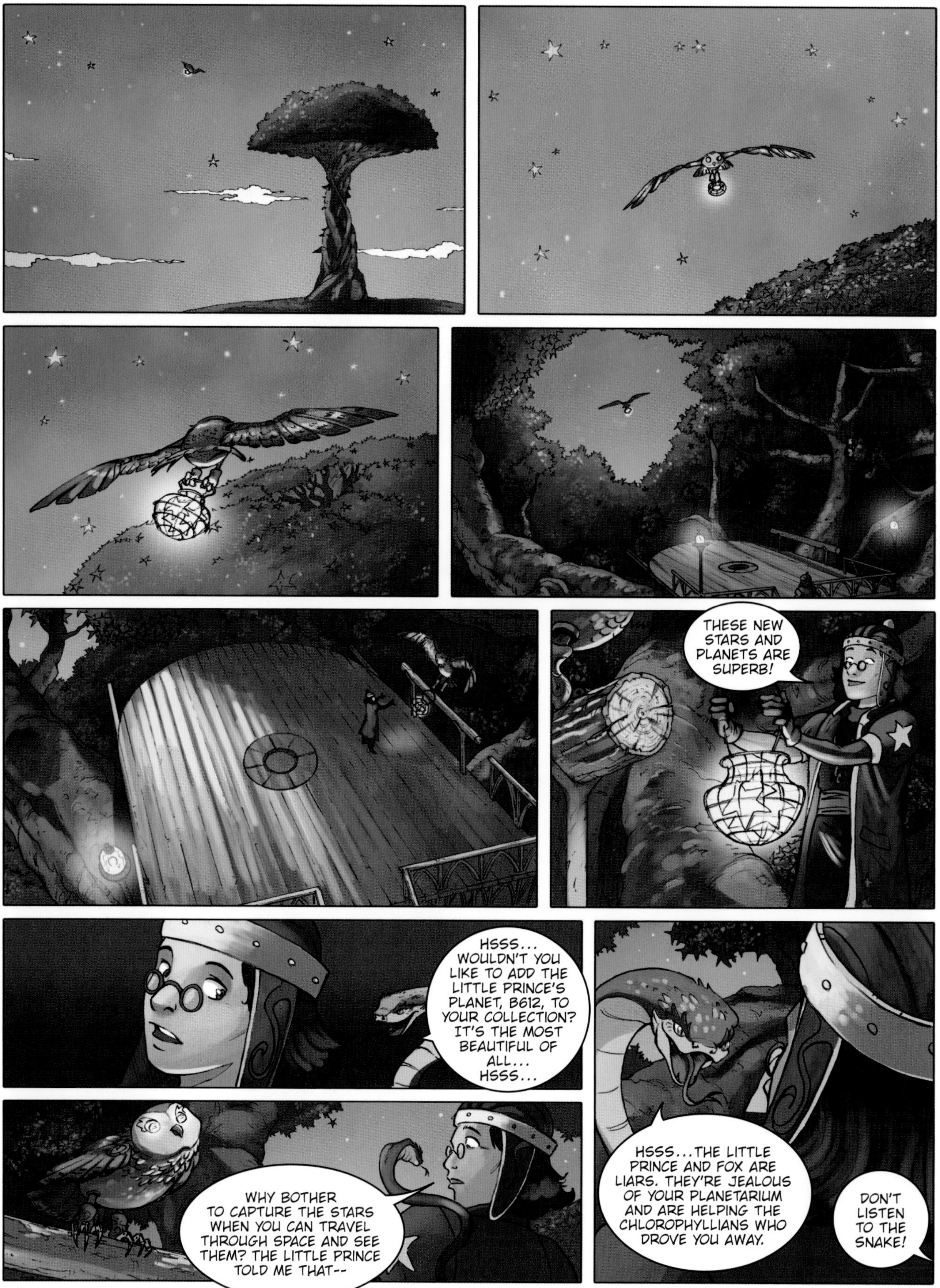
THESE NEW STARS AND PLANETS ARE SUPERB!
HSSS... WOULDN'T YOU LIKE TO ADD THE LITTLE PRINCE'S PLANET, B612, TO YOUR COLLECTION? IT'S THE MOST BEAUTIFUL OF ALL... HSSS...
HSSS... THE LITTLE PRINCE AND FOX ARE LIARS. THEY'RE JEALOUS OF YOUR PLANETARIUM AND ARE HELPING THE CHLOROPHYLLIANS WHO DROVE YOU AWAY.
WHY BOTHER TO CAPTURE THE STARS WHEN YOU CAN TRAVEL THROUGH SPACE AND SEE THEM? THE LITTLE PRINCE TOLD ME THAT--
DON'T LISTEN TO THE SNAKE!

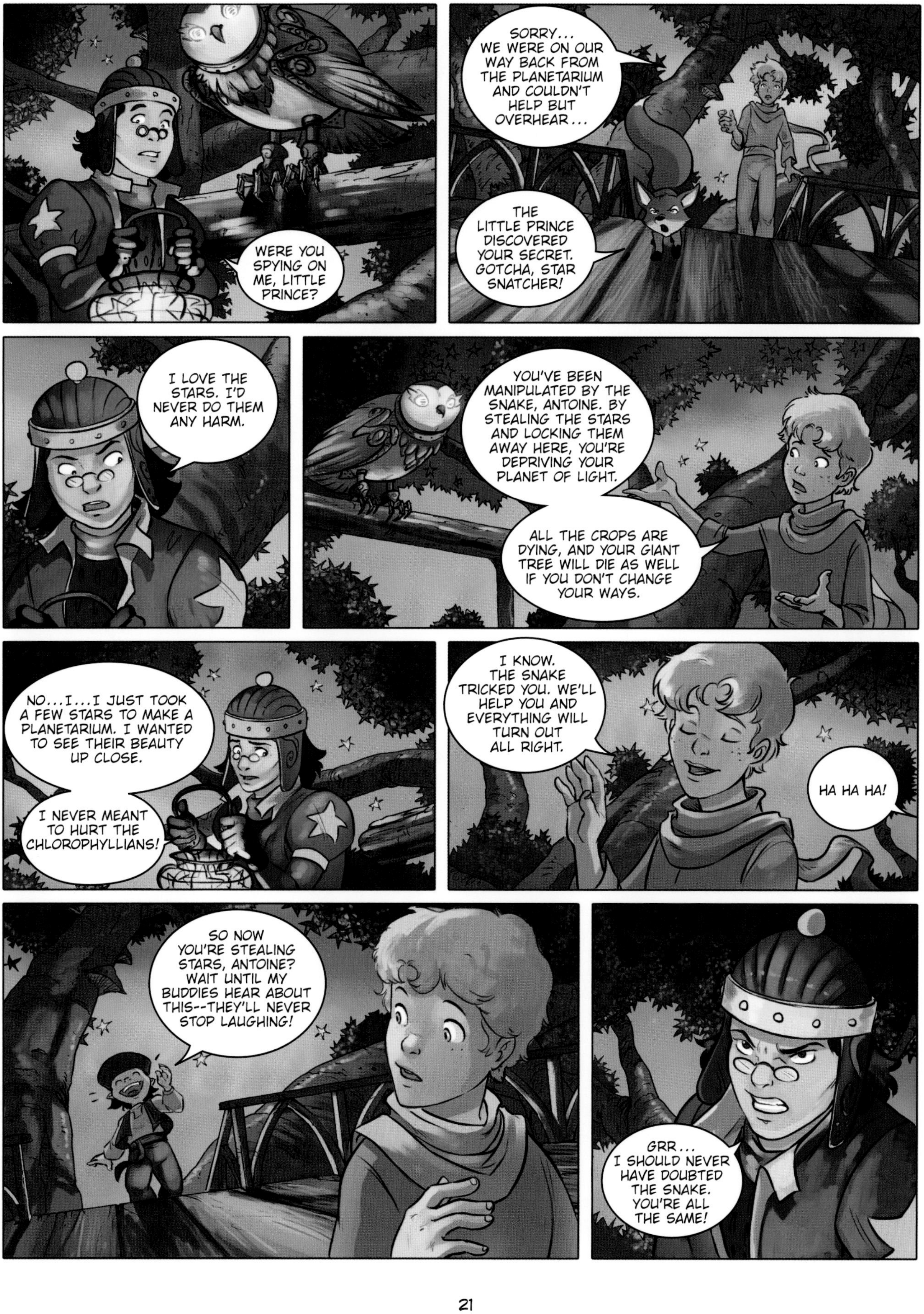
WERE YOU SPYING ON ME, LITTLE PRINCE?
SORRY... WE WERE ON OUR WAY BACK FROM THE PLANETARIUM AND COULDN'T HELP BUT OVERHEAR...
THE LITTLE PRINCE DISCOVERED YOUR SECRET. GOTCHA, STAR SNATCHER!
I LOVE THE STARS. I'D NEVER DO THEM ANY HARM.
YOU'VE BEEN MANIPULATED BY THE SNAKE, ANTOINE. BY STEALING THE STARS AND LOCKING THEM AWAY HERE, YOU'RE DEPRIVING YOUR PLANET OF LIGHT.
ALL THE CROPS ARE DYING, AND YOUR GIANT TREE WILL DIE AS WELL IF YOU DON'T CHANGE YOUR WAYS.
NO...I...I JUST TOOK A FEW STARS TO MAKE A PLANETARIUM. I WANTED TO SEE THEIR BEAUTY UP CLOSE.
I NEVER MEANT TO HURT THE CHLOROPHYLLIANS!
I KNOW. THE SNAKE TRICKED YOU. WE'LL HELP YOU AND EVERYTHING WILL TURN OUT ALL RIGHT.
HA HA HA!
SO NOW YOU'RE STEALING STARS, ANTOINE? WAIT UNTIL MY BUDDIES HEAR ABOUT THIS--THEY'LL NEVER STOP LAUGHING!
GRR... I SHOULD NEVER HAVE DOUBTED THE SNAKE. YOU'RE ALL THE SAME!

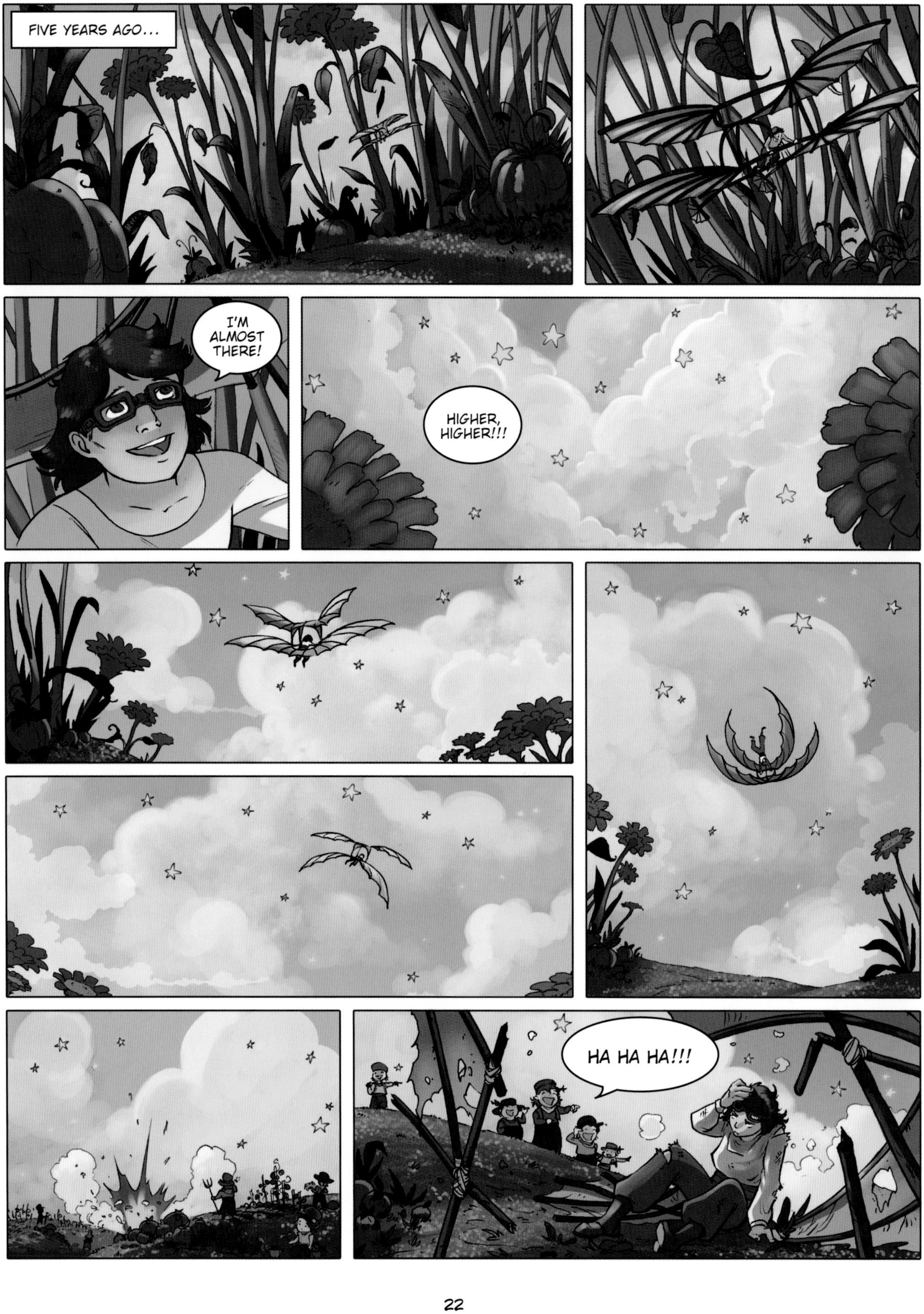
FIVE YEARS AGO...
I'M ALMOST THERE!
HIGHER, HIGHER!!!
HA HA HA!!!

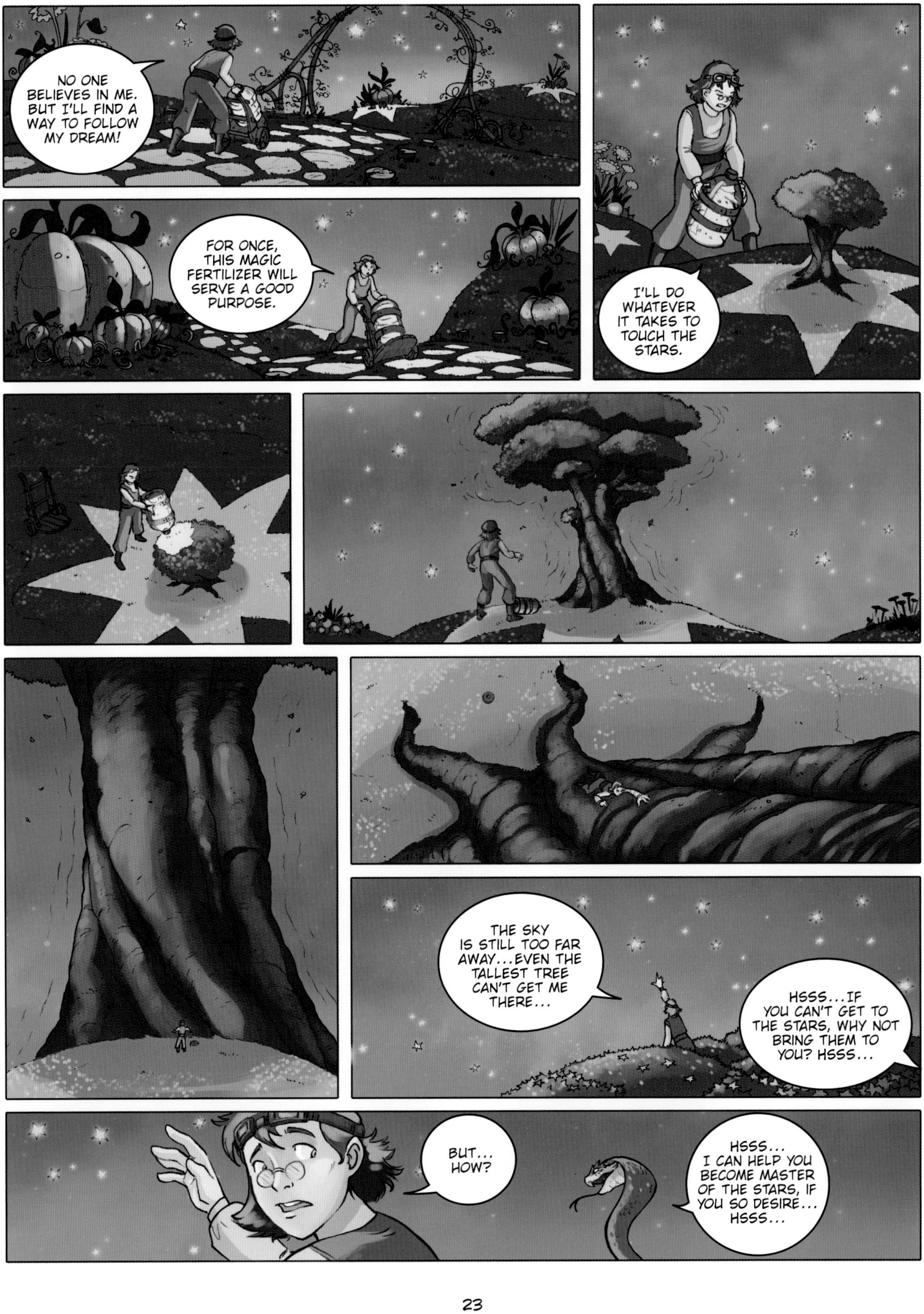
NO ONE BELIEVES IN ME. BUT I'LL FIND A WAY TO FOLLOW MY DREAM!
FOR ONCE, THIS MAGIC FERTILIZER WILL SERVE A GOOD PURPOSE.
I'LL DO WHATEVER IT TAKES TO TOUCH THE STARS.
THE SKY IS STILL TOO FAR AWAY...EVEN THE TALLEST TREE CAN'T GET ME THERE...
HSSS...IF YOU CAN'T GET TO THE STARS, WHY NOT BRING THEM TO YOU? HSSS...
BUT... HOW?
HSSS... I CAN HELP YOU BECOME MASTER OF THE STARS, IF YOU SO DESIRE... HSSS...

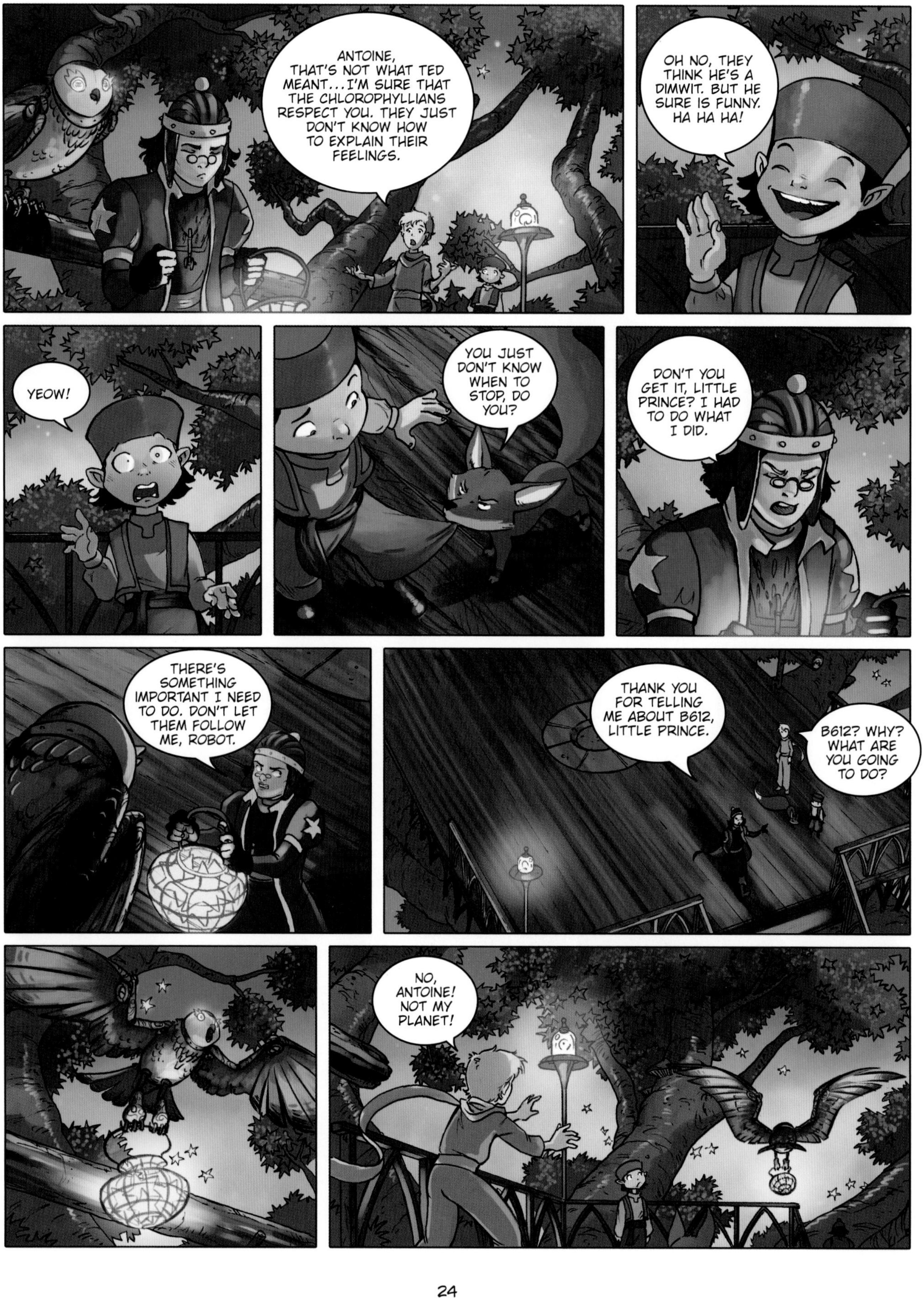
ANTOINE, THAT'S NOT WHAT TED MEANT... I'M SURE THAT THE CHLOROPHYLLIANS RESPECT YOU. THEY JUST DON'T KNOW HOW TO EXPLAIN THEIR FEELINGS.
OH NO, THEY THINK HE'S A DIMWIT. BUT HE SURE IS FUNNY. HA HA HA!
YEOW!
YOU JUST DON'T KNOW WHEN TO STOP, DO YOU?
DON'T YOU GET IT, LITTLE PRINCE? I HAD TO DO WHAT I DID.
THERE'S SOMETHING IMPORTANT I NEED TO DO. DON'T LET THEM FOLLOW ME, ROBOT.
THANK YOU FOR TELLING ME ABOUT B612, LITTLE PRINCE.
B612? WHY? WHAT ARE YOU GOING TO DO?
NO, ANTOINE! NOT MY PLANET!

ANIMALS, YES, BUT I HAVE NO POWER OVER A ROBOT.

LITTLE PRINCE, YOU CAN TALK TO ANIMALS. DO SOMETHING!

ANTOINE'S LOCKED HIMSELF IN THE OBSERVATORY. YOU HAVE TO STOP HIM.

YES... YES, YOU'RE RIGHT.

I'M REALLY SORRY, LITTLE PRINCE. I DIDN'T THINK THAT--

I KNOW, TED. I KNOW.

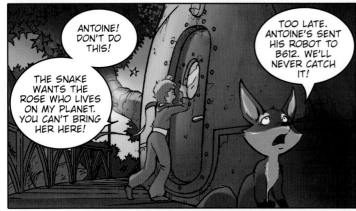

ANTOINE! DON'T DO THIS!

THE SNAKE WANTS THE ROSE WHO LIVES ON MY PLANET. YOU CAN'T BRING HER HERE!

TOO LATE. ANTOINE'S SENT HIS ROBOT TO B612. WE'LL NEVER CATCH IT!

HEY, I DON'T KNOW IF THIS WILL HELP, BUT WHEN I WAS RESTING IN THE OBSERVATORY A LITTLE WHILE AGO...

...I SAW HOW ANTOINE CONTROLS THAT OWL ROBOT. IF WE CAN GET TO THE TOP OF THE TREE, I KNOW HOW TO STOP IT.

GOOD JOB, TED!

ABOUT TIME YOU HELPED!

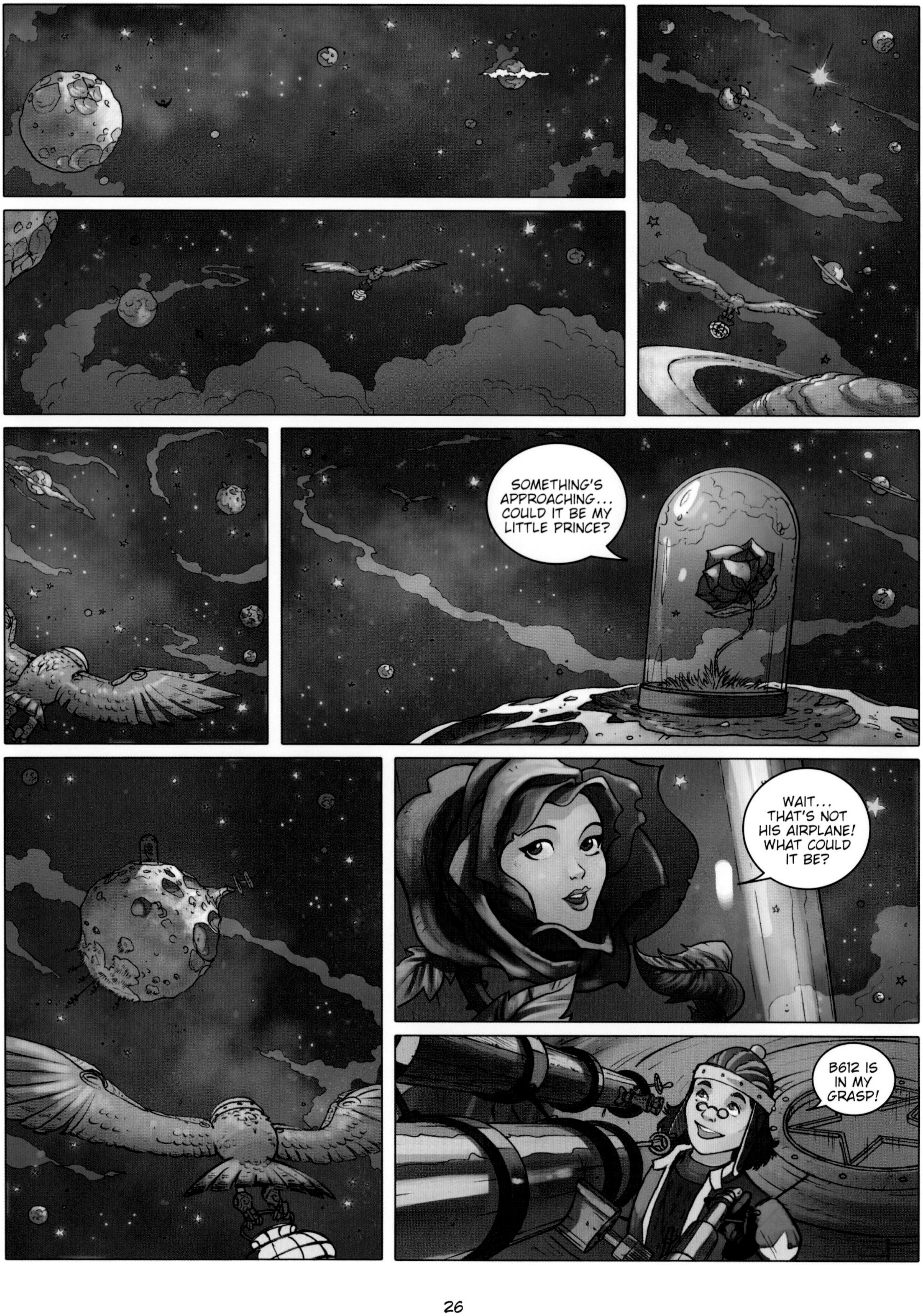
SOMETHING'S APPROACHING... COULD IT BE MY LITTLE PRINCE?
WAIT... THAT'S NOT HIS AIRPLANE! WHAT COULD IT BE?
B612 IS IN MY GRASP!

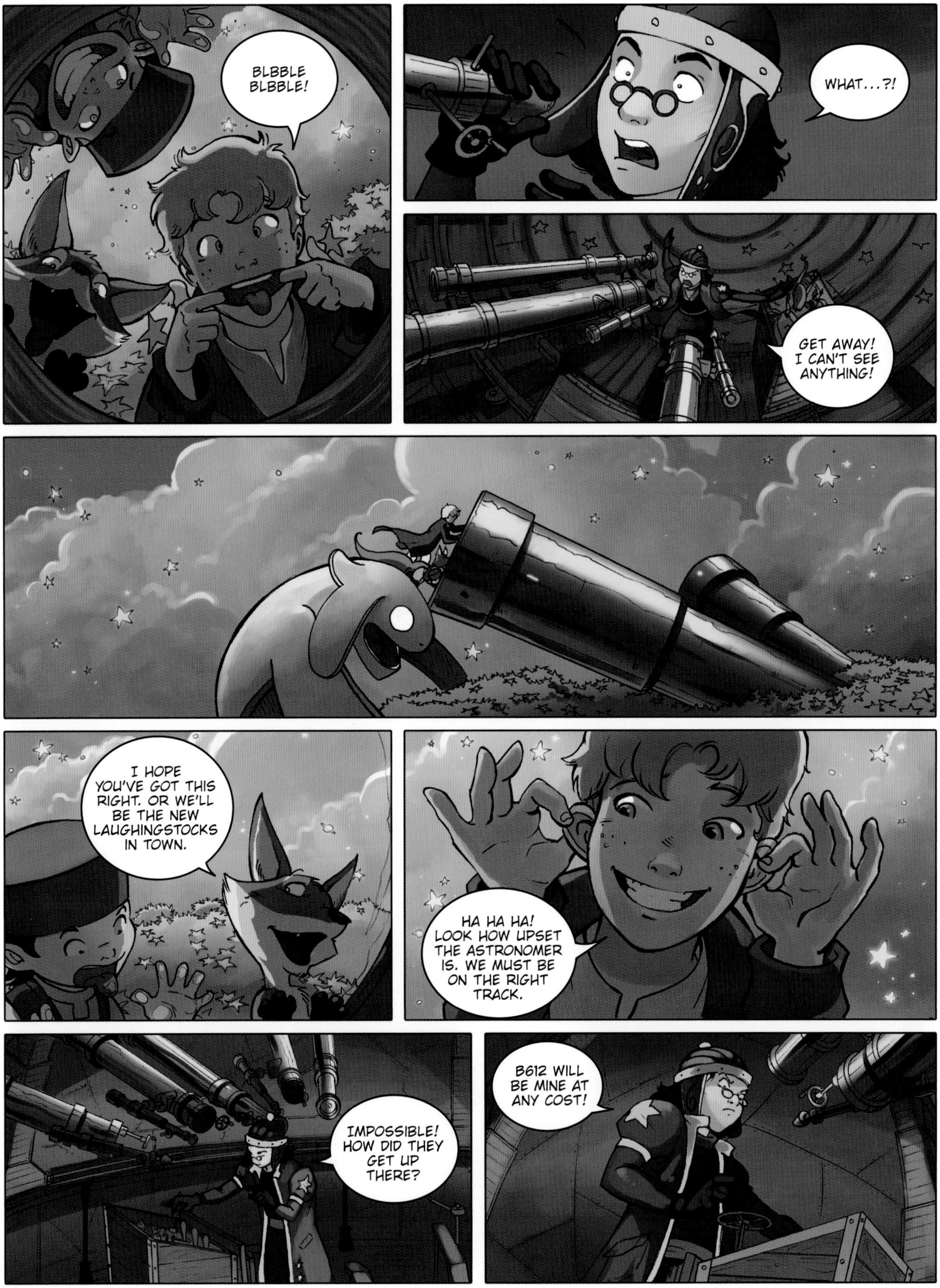

BLBBLE BLBBLE!
WHAT...?!
GET AWAY! I CAN'T SEE ANYTHING!
I HOPE YOU'VE GOT THIS RIGHT. OR WE'LL BE THE NEW LAUGHINGSTOCKS IN TOWN.
HA HA HA! LOOK HOW UPSET THE ASTRONOMER IS. WE MUST BE ON THE RIGHT TRACK.
IMPOSSIBLE! HOW DID THEY GET UP THERE?
B612 WILL BE MINE AT ANY COST!

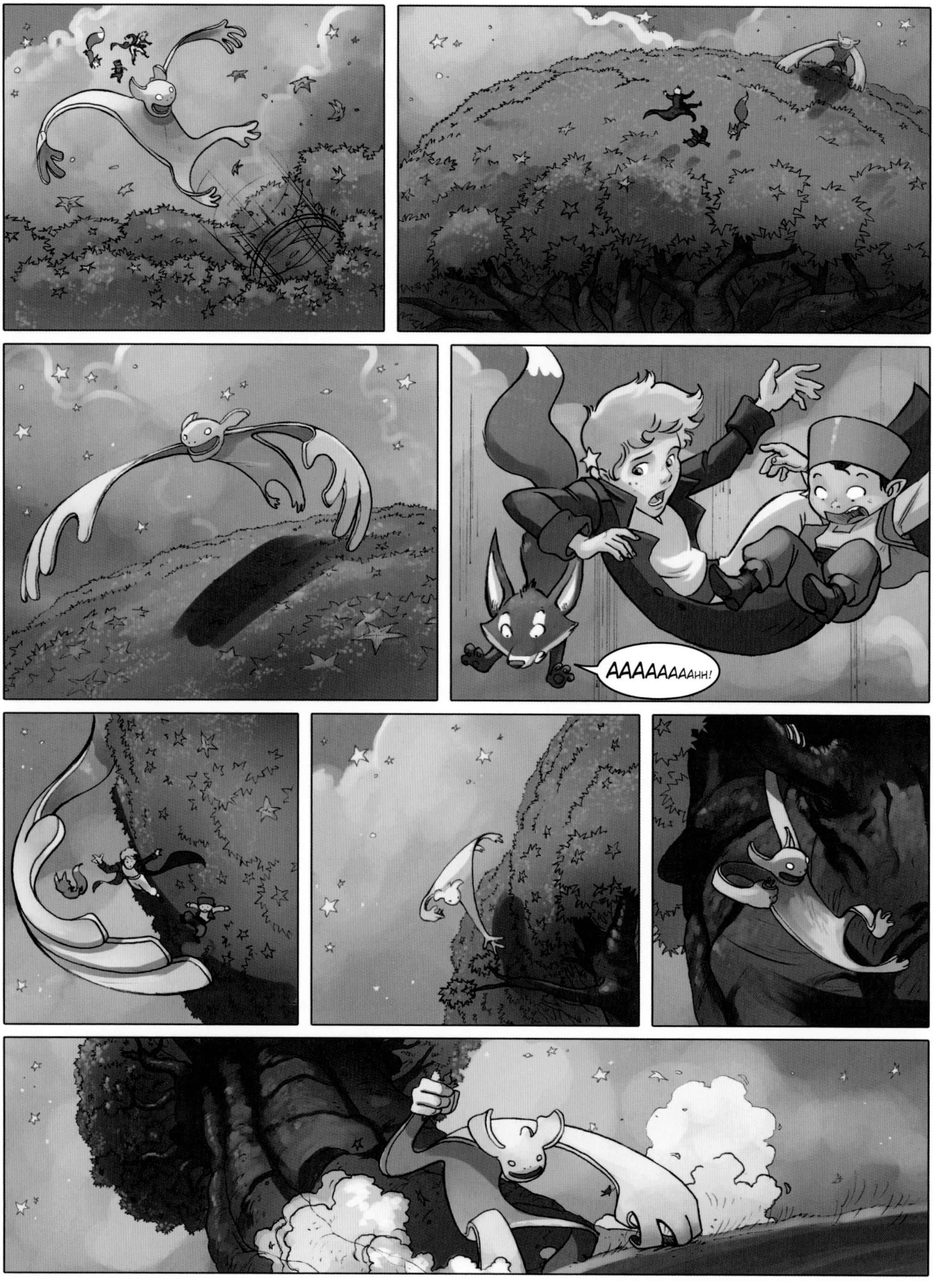
AAAAAAAAHH!

AHH...I CAN SEE CLEARLY NOW.

HELP ME, LITTLE PRINCE!

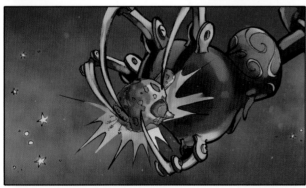

VICTORY IS MINE!

FINALLY. I HAVE WON AT LAST.

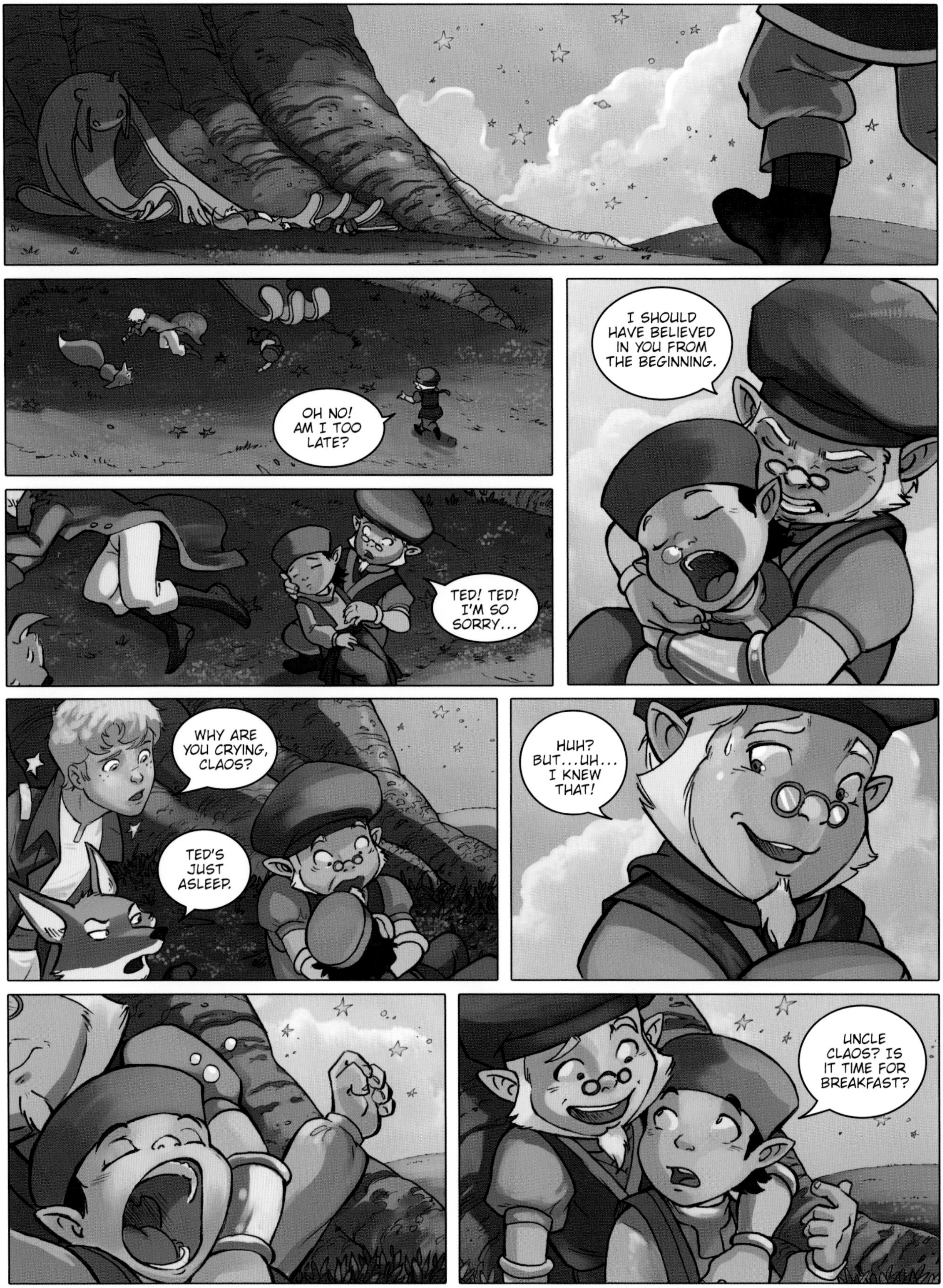
OH NO! AM I TOO LATE?
I SHOULD HAVE BELIEVED IN YOU FROM THE BEGINNING.
TED! TED! I'M SO SORRY...
WHY ARE YOU CRYING, CLAOS?
TED'S JUST ASLEEP.
HUH? BUT...UH... I KNEW THAT!
UNCLE CLAOS? IS IT TIME FOR BREAKFAST?

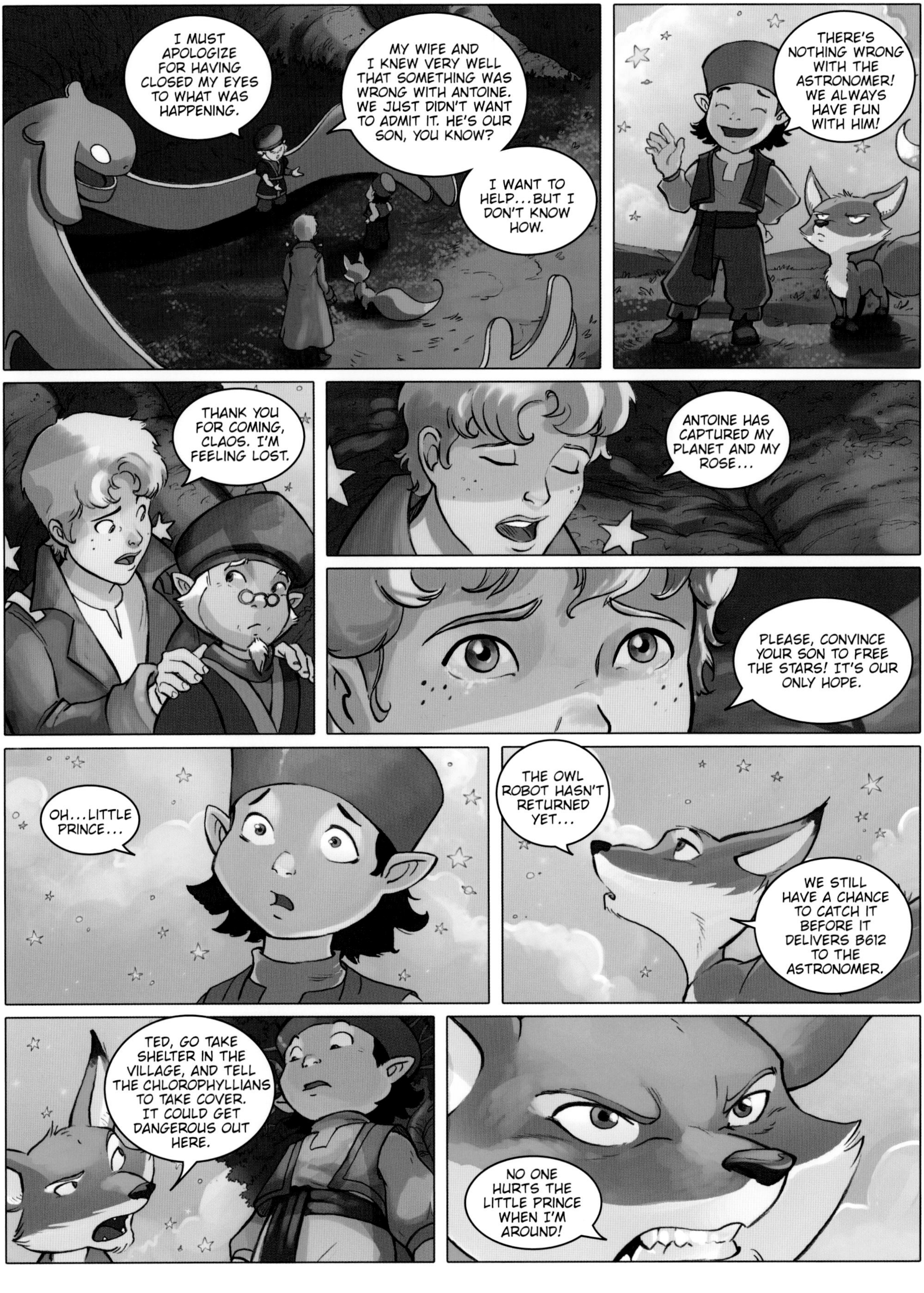
I MUST APOLOGIZE FOR HAVING CLOSED MY EYES TO WHAT WAS HAPPENING.
MY WIFE AND I KNEW VERY WELL THAT SOMETHING WAS WRONG WITH ANTOINE. WE JUST DIDN'T WANT TO ADMIT IT. HE'S OUR SON, YOU KNOW?
I WANT TO HELP...BUT I DON'T KNOW HOW.
THERE'S NOTHING WRONG WITH THE ASTRONOMER! WE ALWAYS HAVE FUN WITH HIM!
THANK YOU FOR COMING, CLAOS. I'M FEELING LOST.
ANTOINE HAS CAPTURED MY PLANET AND MY ROSE...
PLEASE, CONVINCE YOUR SON TO FREE THE STARS! IT'S OUR ONLY HOPE.
OH...LITTLE PRINCE...
THE OWL ROBOT HASN'T RETURNED YET...
WE STILL HAVE A CHANCE TO CATCH IT BEFORE IT DELIVERS B612 TO THE ASTRONOMER.
TED, GO TAKE SHELTER IN THE VILLAGE, AND TELL THE CHLOROPHYLLIANS TO TAKE COVER. IT COULD GET DANGEROUS OUT HERE.
NO ONE HURTS THE LITTLE PRINCE WHEN I'M AROUND!

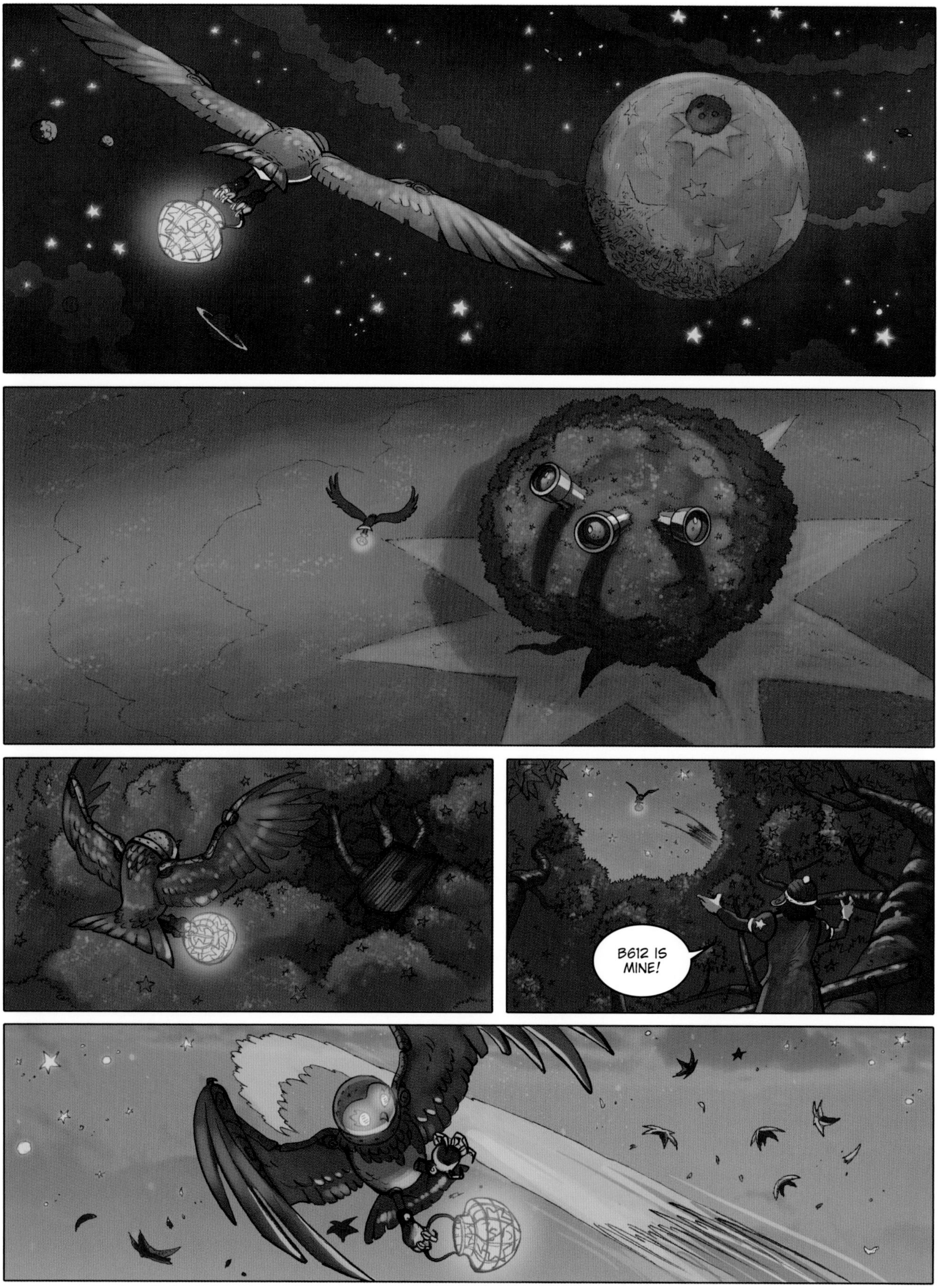
B612 IS
MINE!

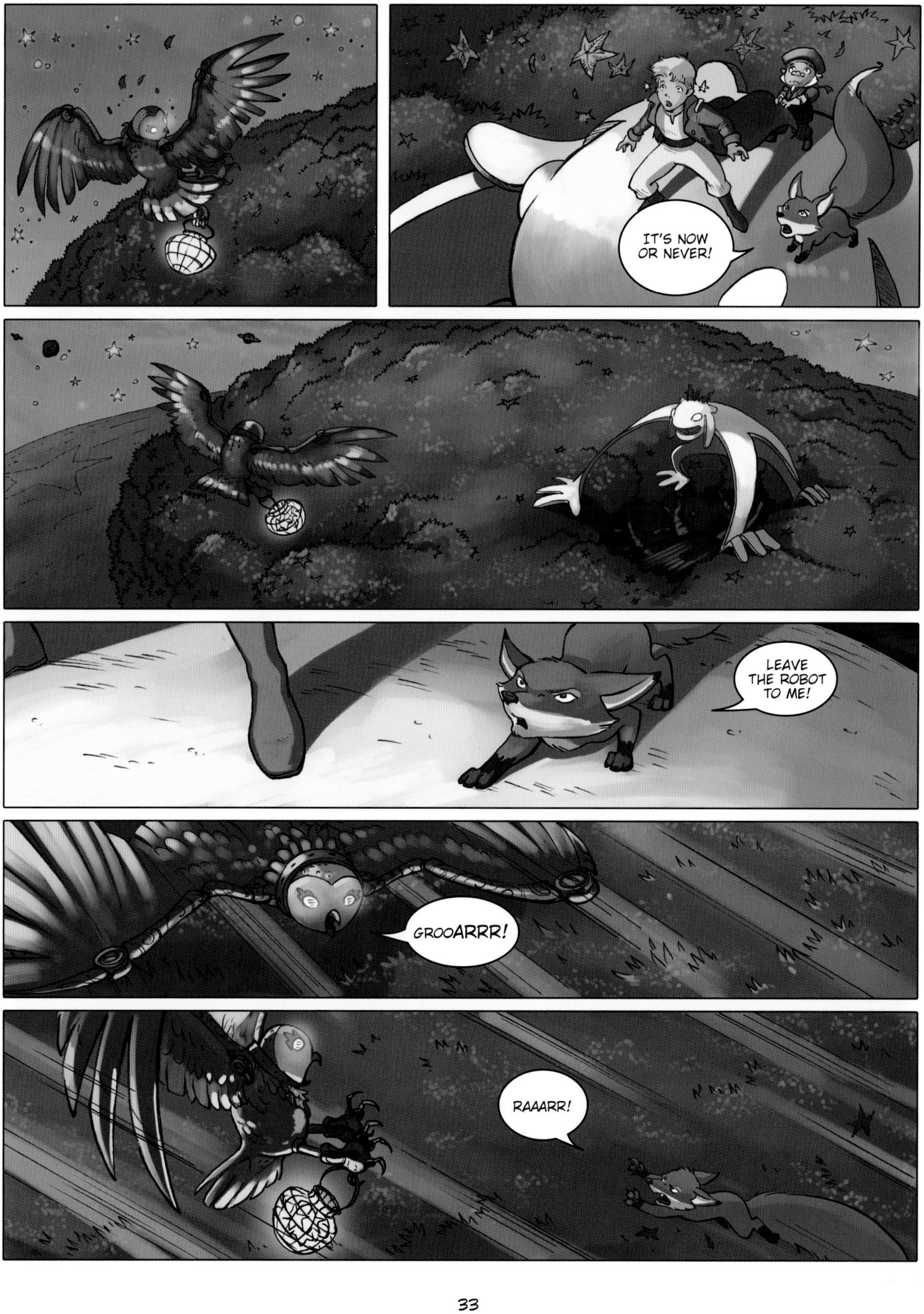
IT'S NOW OR NEVER!
LEAVE THE ROBOT TO ME!
GROOARRR!
RAAARR!

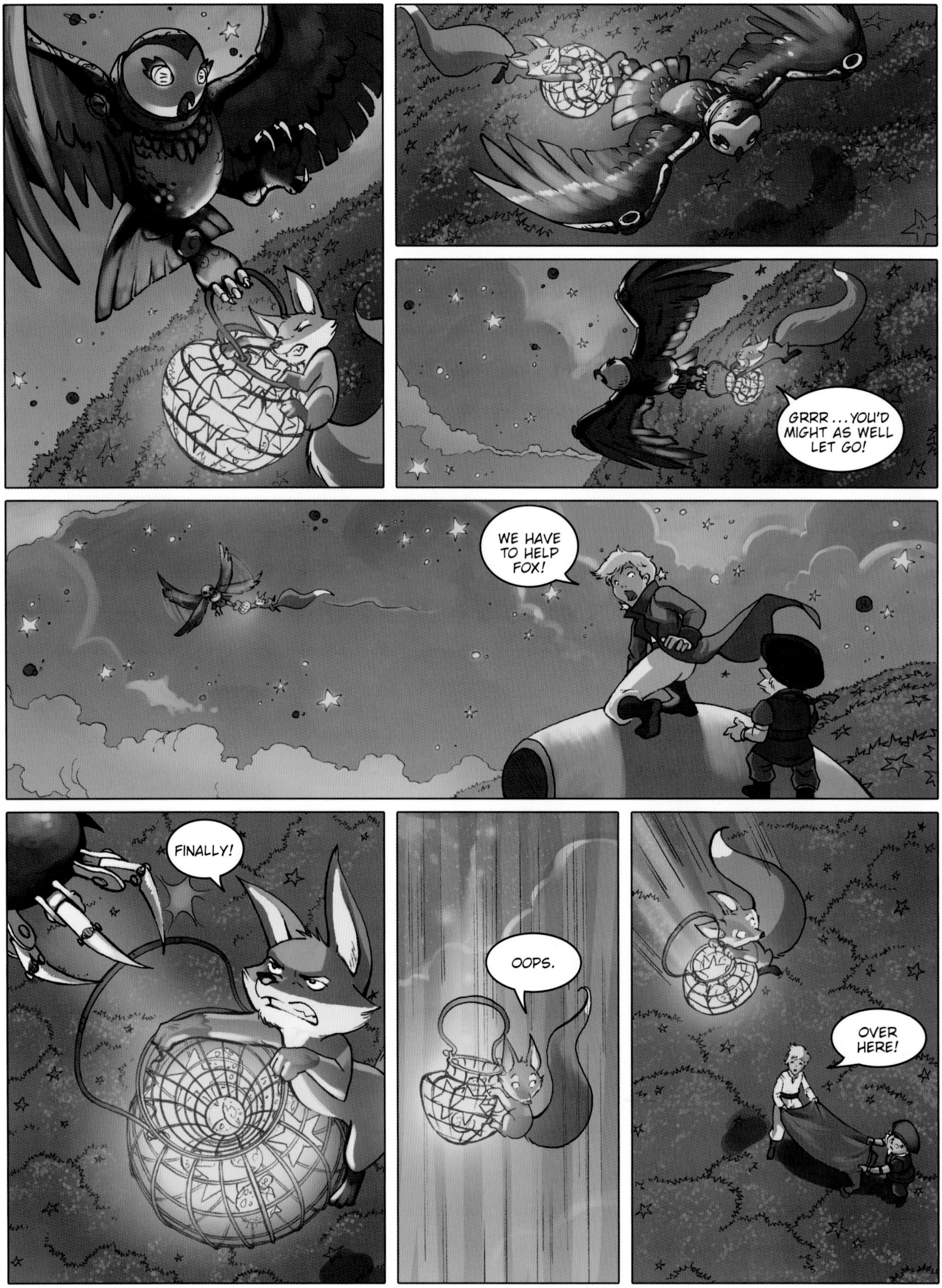
GRRR...YOU'D MIGHT AS WELL LET GO!
WE HAVE TO HELP FOX!
FINALLY!
OOPS.
OVER HERE!

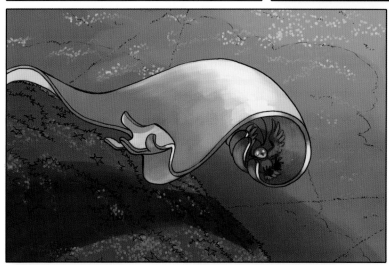

WHAT ABOUT YOUR FRIEND?

DON'T WORRY, HE'LL BE FINE. HE'S MADE OF MAGIC.

THANK YOU, FOX. YOU'VE SAVED MY ROSE.

MEH. I'D RATHER KEEP ALL MY PAWS ON THE GROUND.

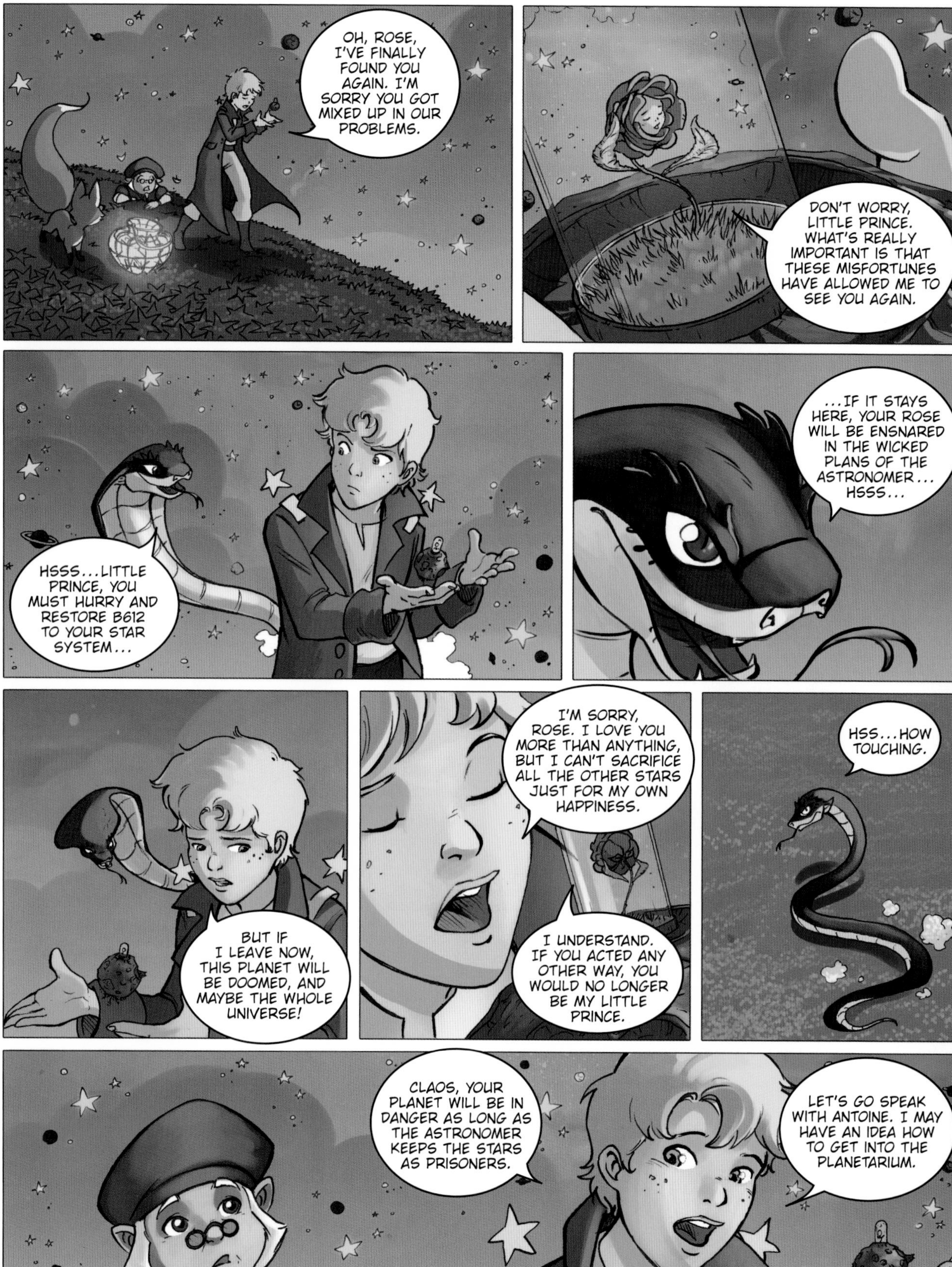
OH, ROSE, I'VE FINALLY FOUND YOU AGAIN. I'M SORRY YOU GOT MIXED UP IN OUR PROBLEMS.
DON'T WORRY, LITTLE PRINCE. WHAT'S REALLY IMPORTANT IS THAT THESE MISFORTUNES HAVE ALLOWED ME TO SEE YOU AGAIN.
HSSS...LITTLE PRINCE, YOU MUST HURRY AND RESTORE B612 TO YOUR STAR SYSTEM...
...IF IT STAYS HERE, YOUR ROSE WILL BE ENSNARED IN THE WICKED PLANS OF THE ASTRONOMER... HSSS...
BUT IF I LEAVE NOW, THIS PLANET WILL BE DOOMED, AND MAYBE THE WHOLE UNIVERSE!
I'M SORRY, ROSE. I LOVE YOU MORE THAN ANYTHING, BUT I CAN'T SACRIFICE ALL THE OTHER STARS JUST FOR MY OWN HAPPINESS.
I UNDERSTAND. IF YOU ACTED ANY OTHER WAY, YOU WOULD NO LONGER BE MY LITTLE PRINCE.
HSS...HOW TOUCHING.
CLAOS, YOUR PLANET WILL BE IN DANGER AS LONG AS THE ASTRONOMER KEEPS THE STARS AS PRISONERS.
LET'S GO SPEAK WITH ANTOINE. I MAY HAVE AN IDEA HOW TO GET INTO THE PLANETARIUM.

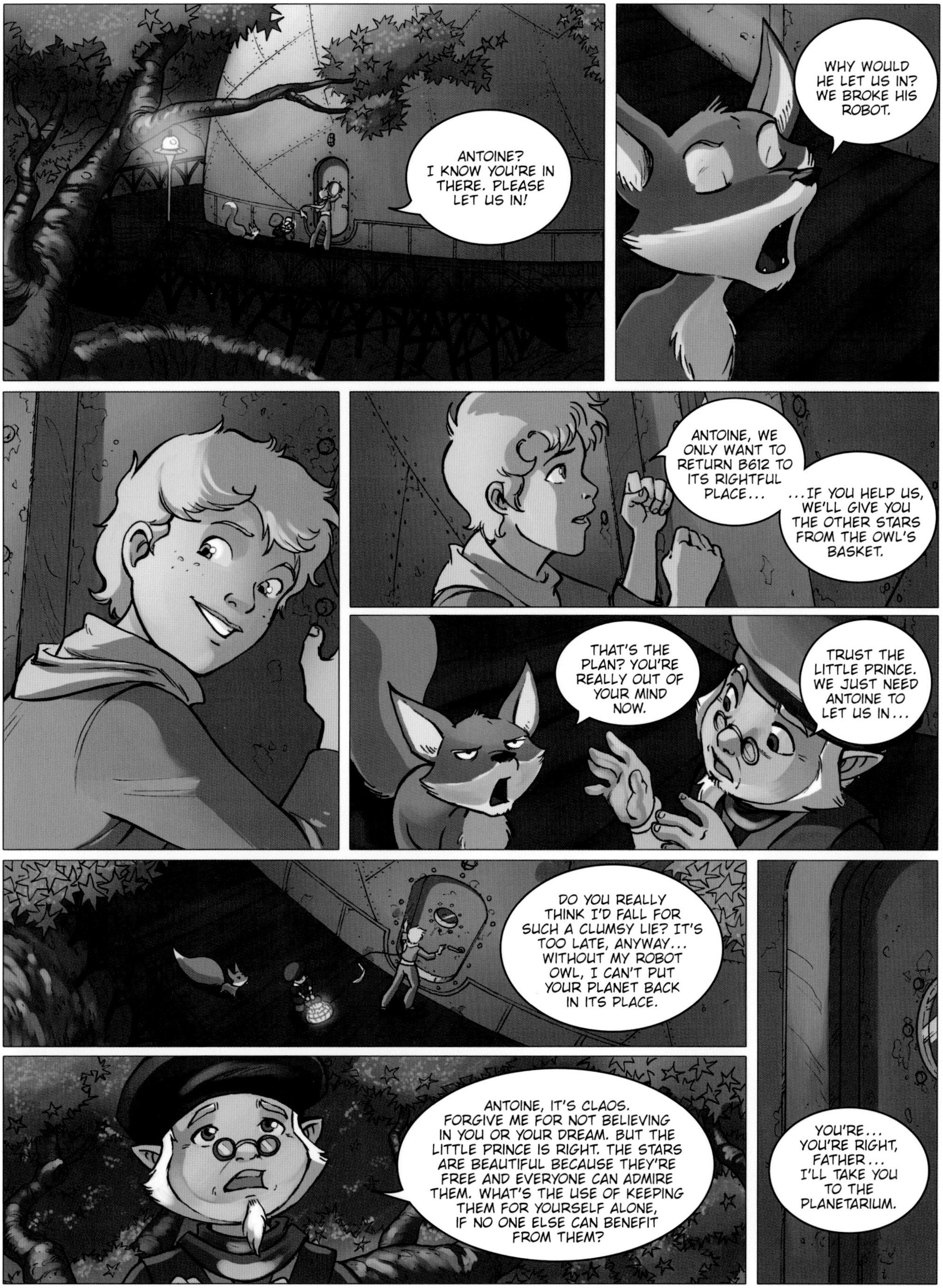
ANTOINE? I KNOW YOU'RE IN THERE. PLEASE LET US IN!
WHY WOULD HE LET US IN? WE BROKE HIS ROBOT.
ANTOINE, WE ONLY WANT TO RETURN B612 TO ITS RIGHTFUL PLACE...
...IF YOU HELP US, WE'LL GIVE YOU THE OTHER STARS FROM THE OWL'S BASKET.
THAT'S THE PLAN? YOU'RE REALLY OUT OF YOUR MIND NOW.
TRUST THE LITTLE PRINCE. WE JUST NEED ANTOINE TO LET US IN...
DO YOU REALLY THINK I'D FALL FOR SUCH A CLUMSY LIE? IT'S TOO LATE, ANYWAY... WITHOUT MY ROBOT OWL, I CAN'T PUT YOUR PLANET BACK IN ITS PLACE.
ANTOINE, IT'S CLAOS. FORGIVE ME FOR NOT BELIEVING IN YOU OR YOUR DREAM. BUT THE LITTLE PRINCE IS RIGHT. THE STARS ARE BEAUTIFUL BECAUSE THEY'RE FREE AND EVERYONE CAN ADMIRE THEM. WHAT'S THE USE OF KEEPING THEM FOR YOURSELF ALONE, IF NO ONE ELSE CAN BENEFIT FROM THEM?
YOU'RE... YOU'RE RIGHT, FATHER... I'LL TAKE YOU TO THE PLANETARIUM.

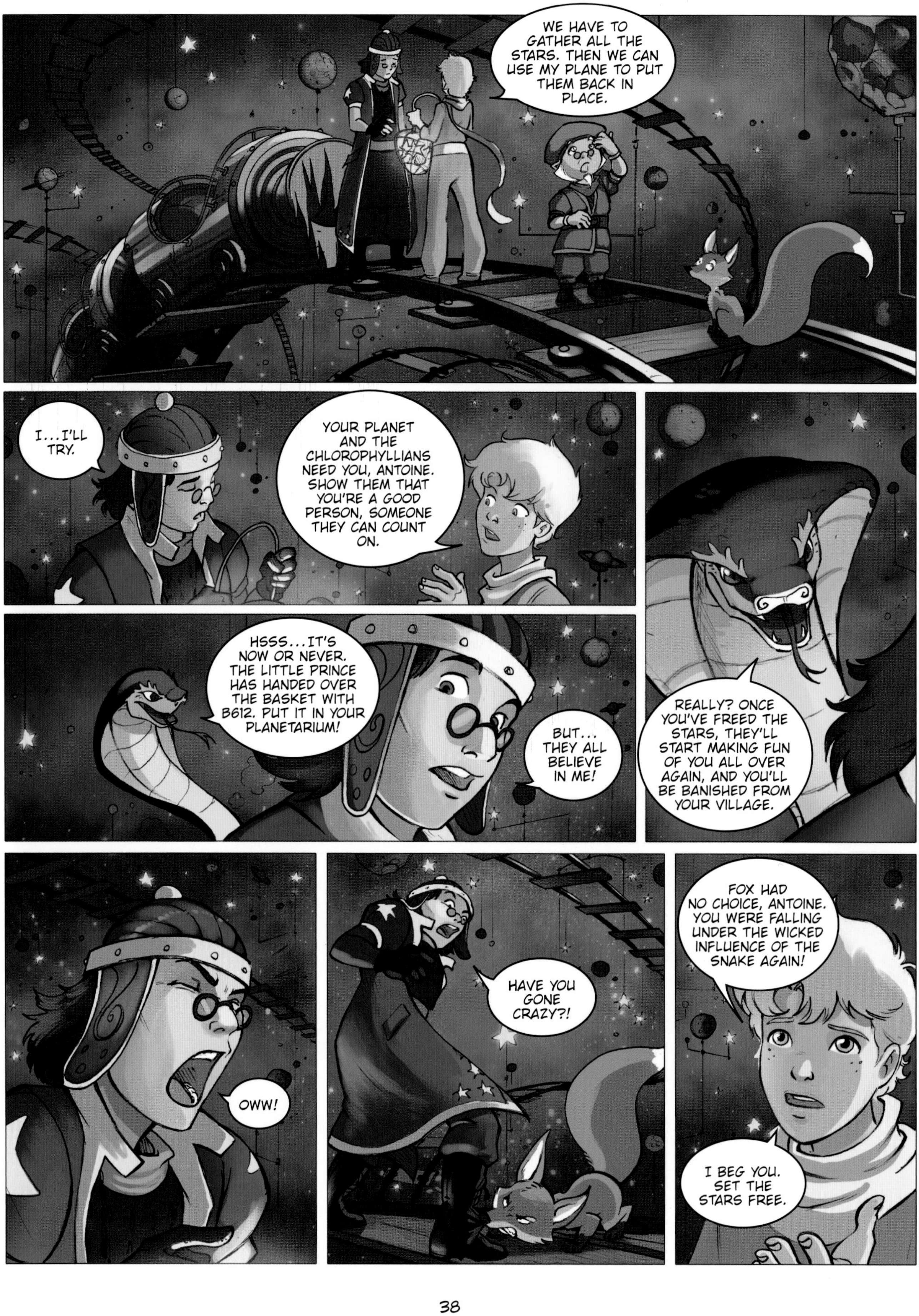
WE HAVE TO GATHER ALL THE STARS. THEN WE CAN USE MY PLANE TO PUT THEM BACK IN PLACE.
I...I'LL TRY.
YOUR PLANET AND THE CHLOROPHYLLIANS NEED YOU, ANTOINE. SHOW THEM THAT YOU'RE A GOOD PERSON, SOMEONE THEY CAN COUNT ON.
HSSS...IT'S NOW OR NEVER. THE LITTLE PRINCE HAS HANDED OVER THE BASKET WITH B612. PUT IT IN YOUR PLANETARIUM!
BUT... THEY ALL BELIEVE IN ME!
REALLY? ONCE YOU'VE FREED THE STARS, THEY'LL START MAKING FUN OF YOU ALL OVER AGAIN, AND YOU'LL BE BANISHED FROM YOUR VILLAGE.
OWW!
HAVE YOU GONE CRAZY?!
FOX HAD NO CHOICE, ANTOINE. YOU WERE FALLING UNDER THE WICKED INFLUENCE OF THE SNAKE AGAIN!
I BEG YOU. SET THE STARS FREE.

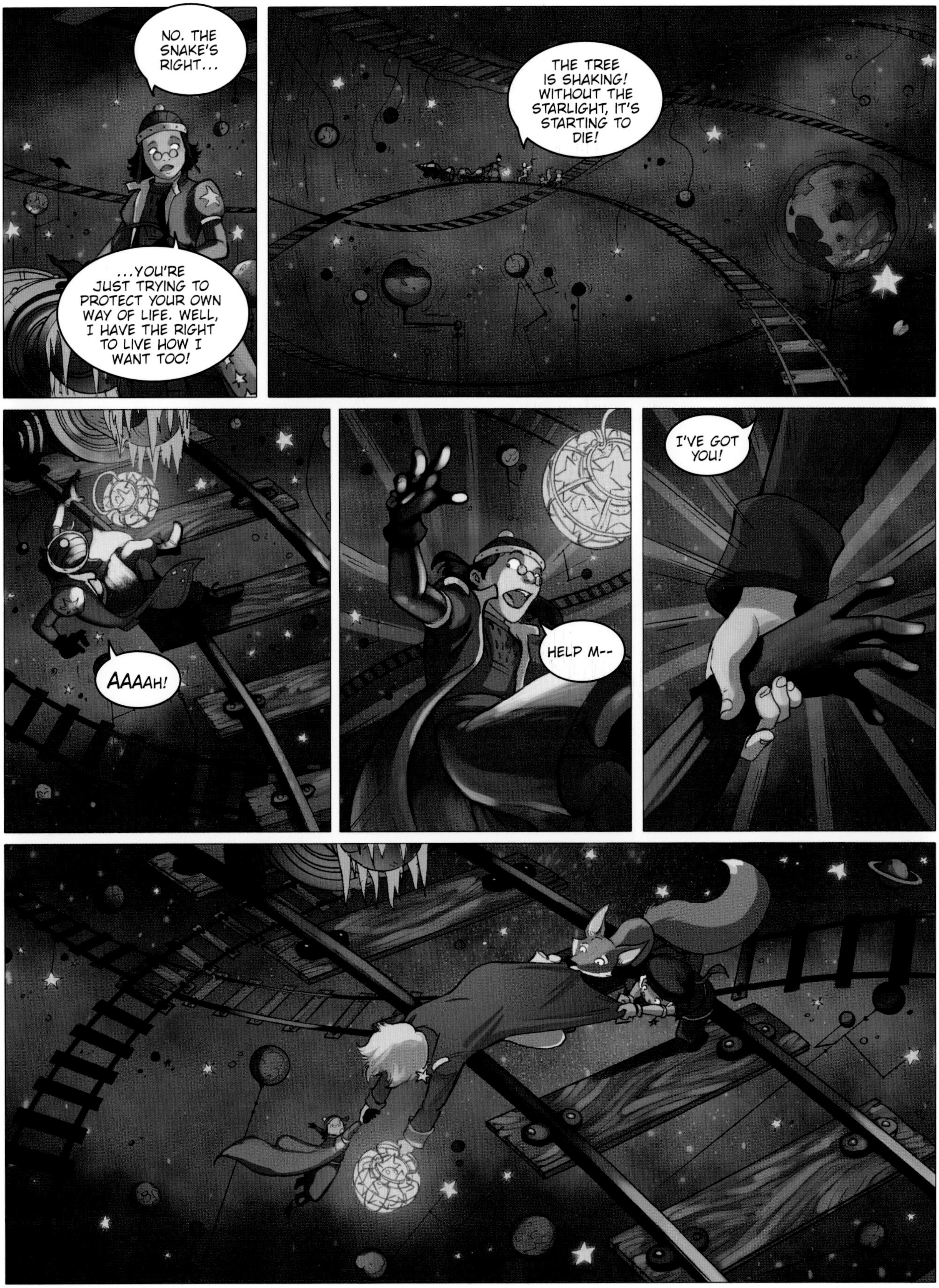

NO. THE SNAKE'S RIGHT...
...YOU'RE JUST TRYING TO PROTECT YOUR OWN WAY OF LIFE. WELL, I HAVE THE RIGHT TO LIVE HOW I WANT TOO!
THE TREE IS SHAKING! WITHOUT THE STARLIGHT, IT'S STARTING TO DIE!
AAAAH!
HELP M--
I'VE GOT YOU!

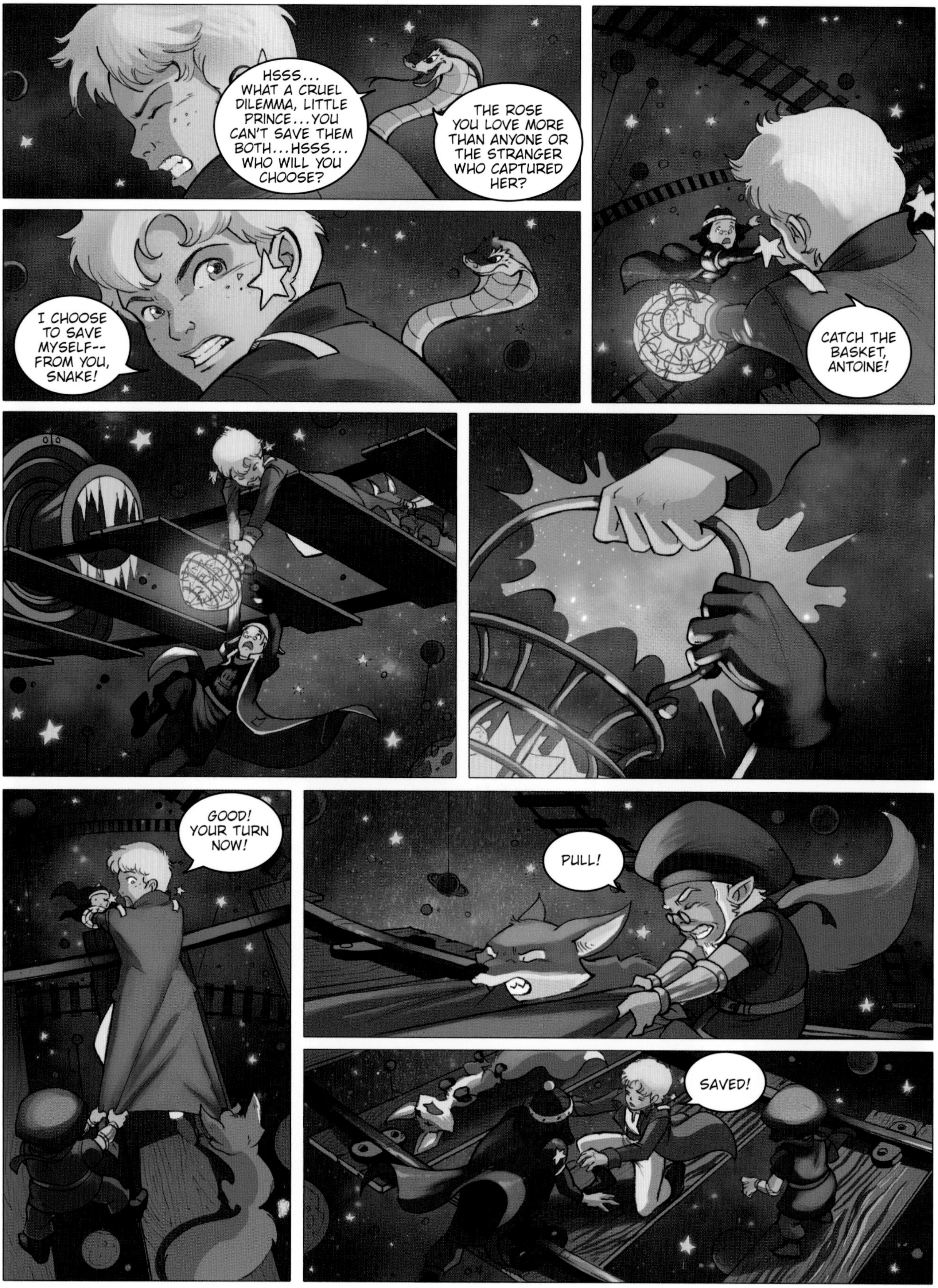
HSSS... WHAT A CRUEL DILEMMA, LITTLE PRINCE...YOU CAN'T SAVE THEM BOTH...HSSS... WHO WILL YOU CHOOSE?
THE ROSE YOU LOVE MORE THAN ANYONE OR THE STRANGER WHO CAPTURED HER?
I CHOOSE TO SAVE MYSELF-- FROM YOU, SNAKE!
CATCH THE BASKET, ANTOINE!
GOOD! YOUR TURN NOW!
PULL!
SAVED!

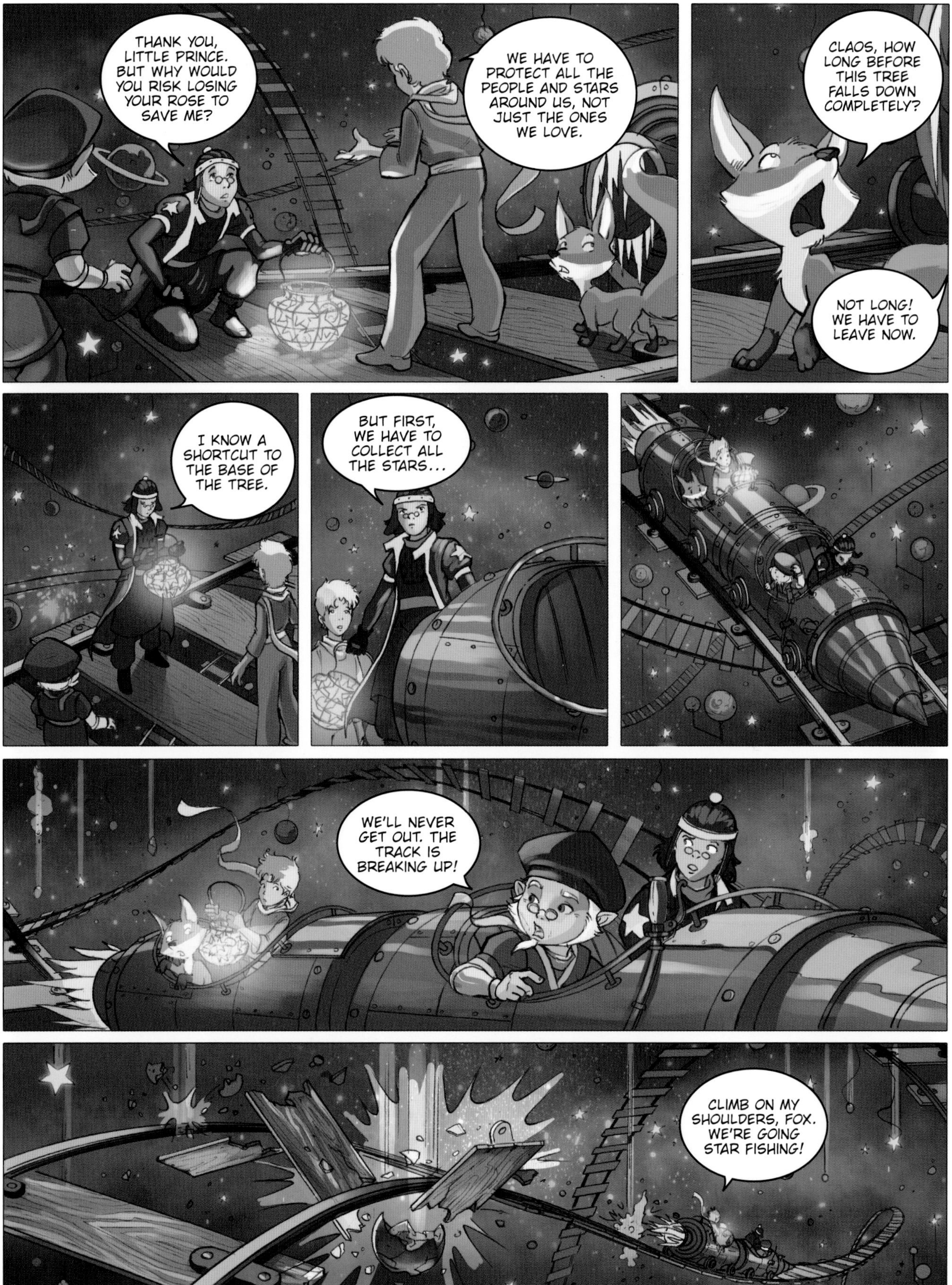
THANK YOU, LITTLE PRINCE. BUT WHY WOULD YOU RISK LOSING YOUR ROSE TO SAVE ME?
WE HAVE TO PROTECT ALL THE PEOPLE AND STARS AROUND US, NOT JUST THE ONES WE LOVE.
CLAOS, HOW LONG BEFORE THIS TREE FALLS DOWN COMPLETELY?
NOT LONG! WE HAVE TO LEAVE NOW.
I KNOW A SHORTCUT TO THE BASE OF THE TREE.
BUT FIRST, WE HAVE TO COLLECT ALL THE STARS...
WE'LL NEVER GET OUT. THE TRACK IS BREAKING UP!
CLIMB ON MY SHOULDERS, FOX. WE'RE GOING STAR FISHING!

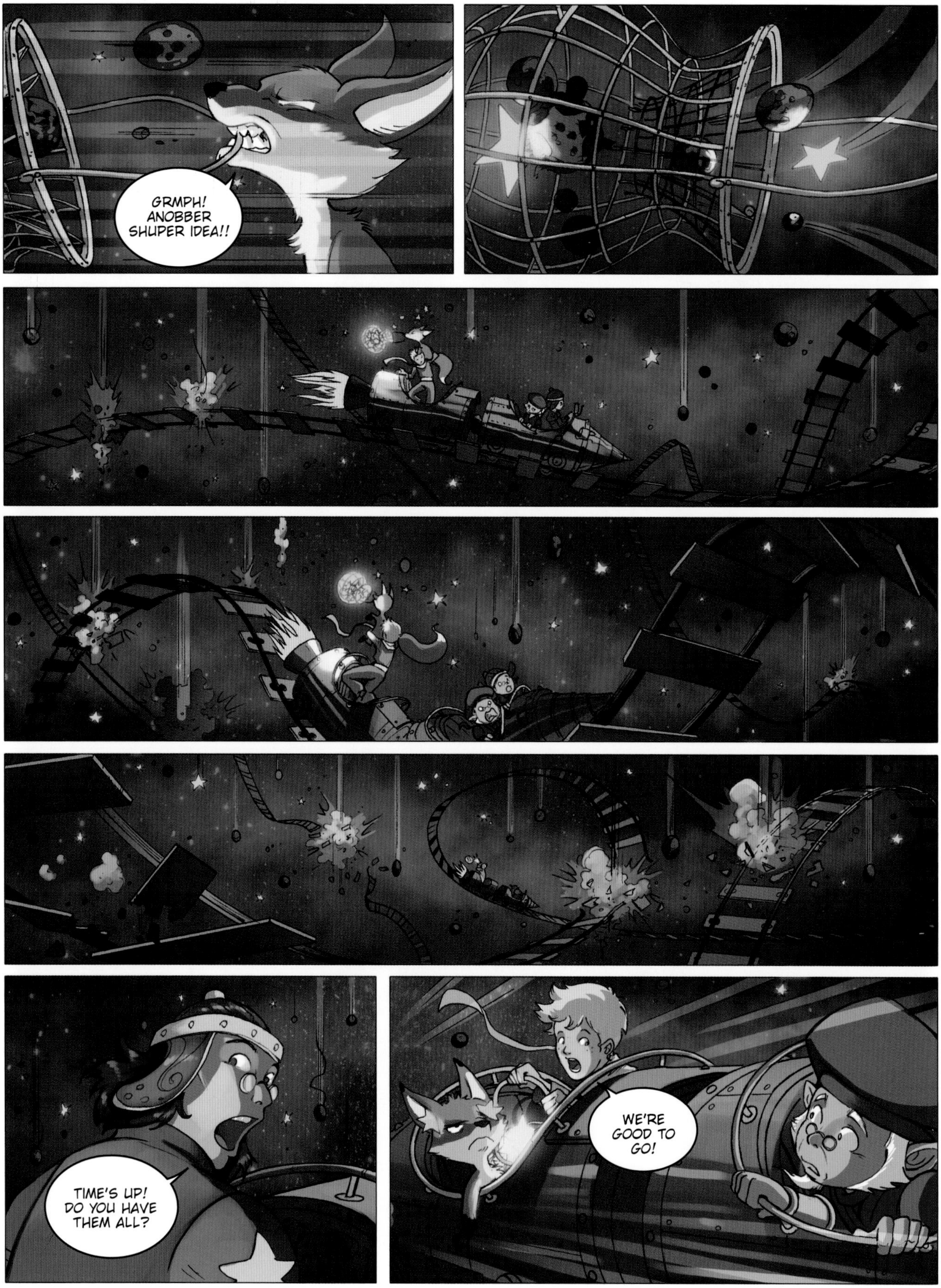
GRMPH! ANOBBER SHUPER IDEA!!
TIME'S UP! DO YOU HAVE THEM ALL?
WE'RE GOOD TO GO!

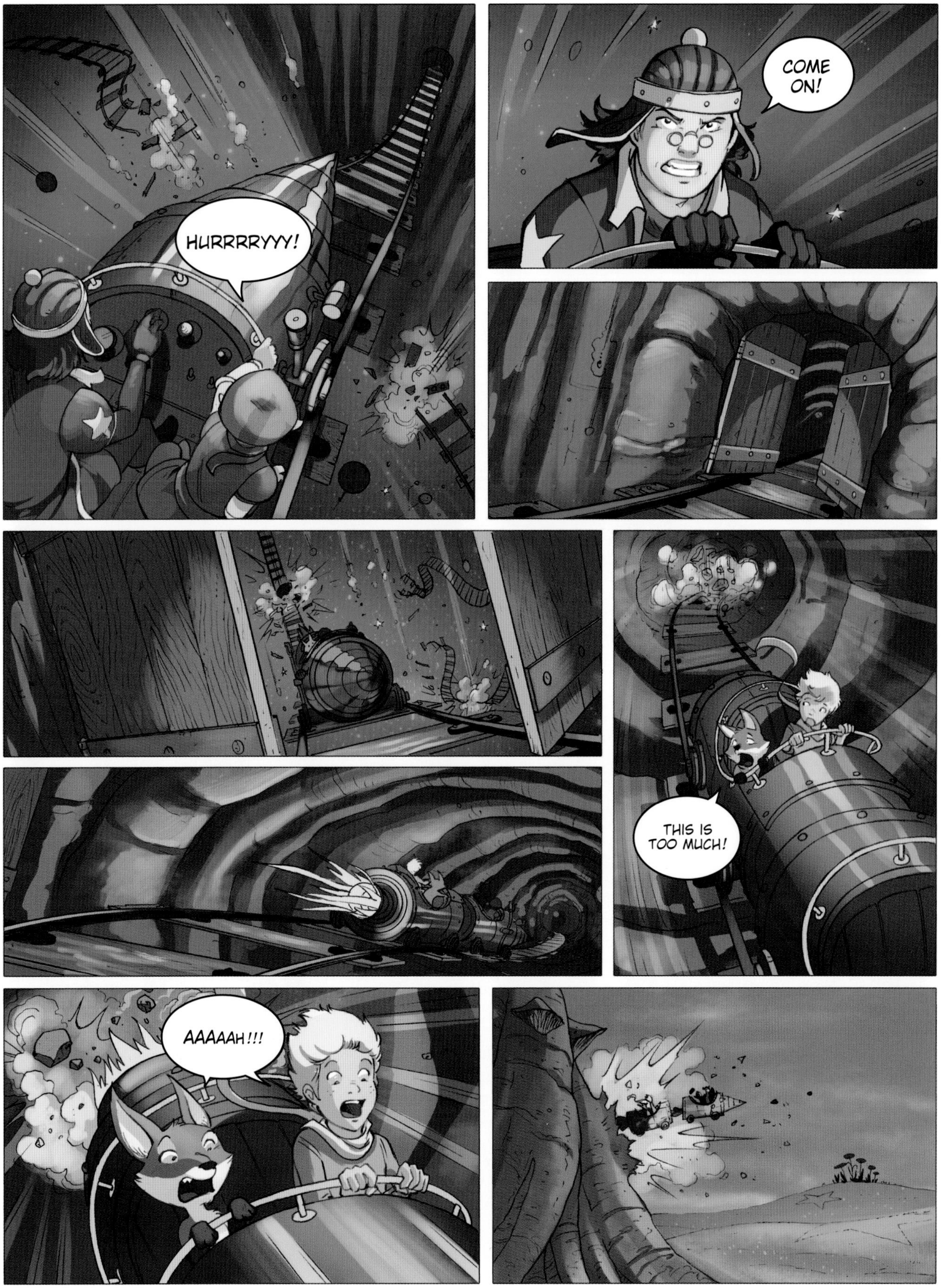
HURRRRYYY!
COME ON!
THIS IS TOO MUCH!
AAAAAH!!!

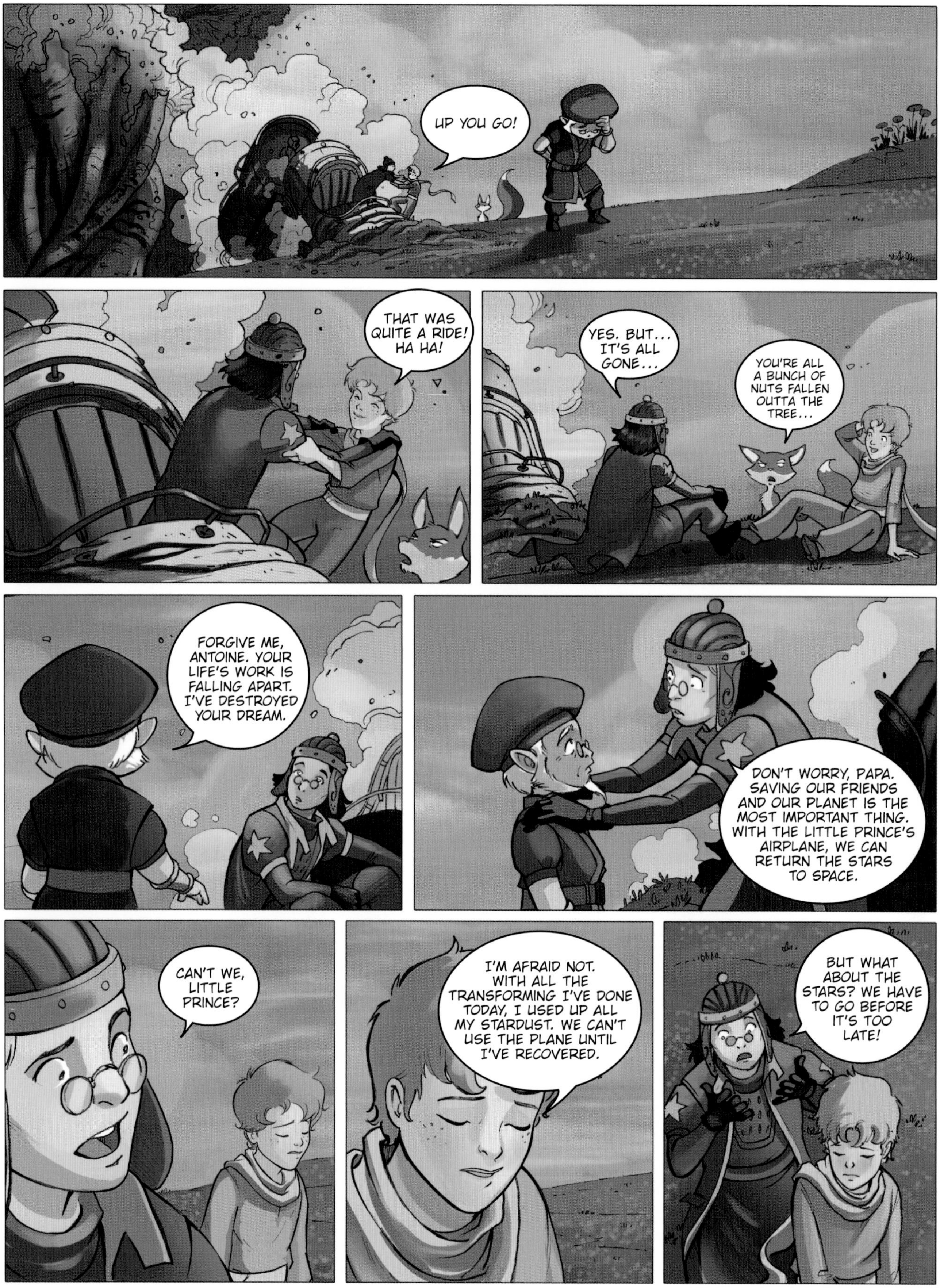
UP YOU GO!
THAT WAS QUITE A RIDE! HA HA!
YES. BUT... IT'S ALL GONE...
YOU'RE ALL A BUNCH OF NUTS FALLEN OUTTA THE TREE...
FORGIVE ME, ANTOINE. YOUR LIFE'S WORK IS FALLING APART. I'VE DESTROYED YOUR DREAM.
DON'T WORRY, PAPA. SAVING OUR FRIENDS AND OUR PLANET IS THE MOST IMPORTANT THING. WITH THE LITTLE PRINCE'S AIRPLANE, WE CAN RETURN THE STARS TO SPACE.
CAN'T WE, LITTLE PRINCE?
I'M AFRAID NOT. WITH ALL THE TRANSFORMING I'VE DONE TODAY, I USED UP ALL MY STARDUST. WE CAN'T USE THE PLANE UNTIL I'VE RECOVERED.
BUT WHAT ABOUT THE STARS? WE HAVE TO GO BEFORE IT'S TOO LATE!

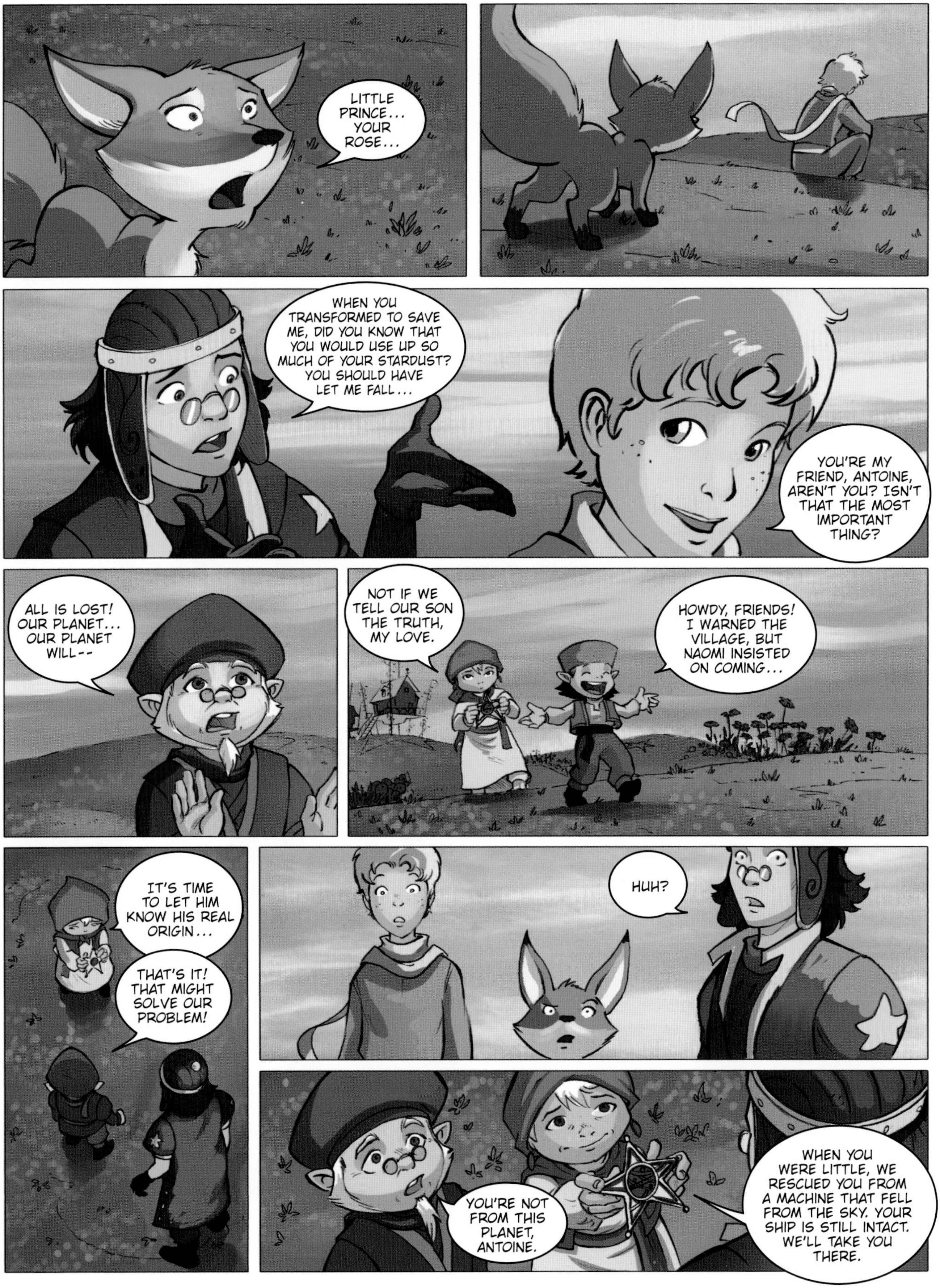
LITTLE PRINCE... YOUR ROSE...
WHEN YOU TRANSFORMED TO SAVE ME, DID YOU KNOW THAT YOU WOULD USE UP SO MUCH OF YOUR STARDUST? YOU SHOULD HAVE LET ME FALL...
YOU'RE MY FRIEND, ANTOINE, AREN'T YOU? ISN'T THAT THE MOST IMPORTANT THING?
ALL IS LOST! OUR PLANET... OUR PLANET WILL--
NOT IF WE TELL OUR SON THE TRUTH, MY LOVE.
HOWDY, FRIENDS! I WARNED THE VILLAGE, BUT NAOMI INSISTED ON COMING...
IT'S TIME TO LET HIM KNOW HIS REAL ORIGIN...
THAT'S IT! THAT MIGHT SOLVE OUR PROBLEM!
HUH?
YOU'RE NOT FROM THIS PLANET, ANTOINE.
WHEN YOU WERE LITTLE, WE RESCUED YOU FROM A MACHINE THAT FELL FROM THE SKY. YOUR SHIP IS STILL INTACT. WE'LL TAKE YOU THERE.

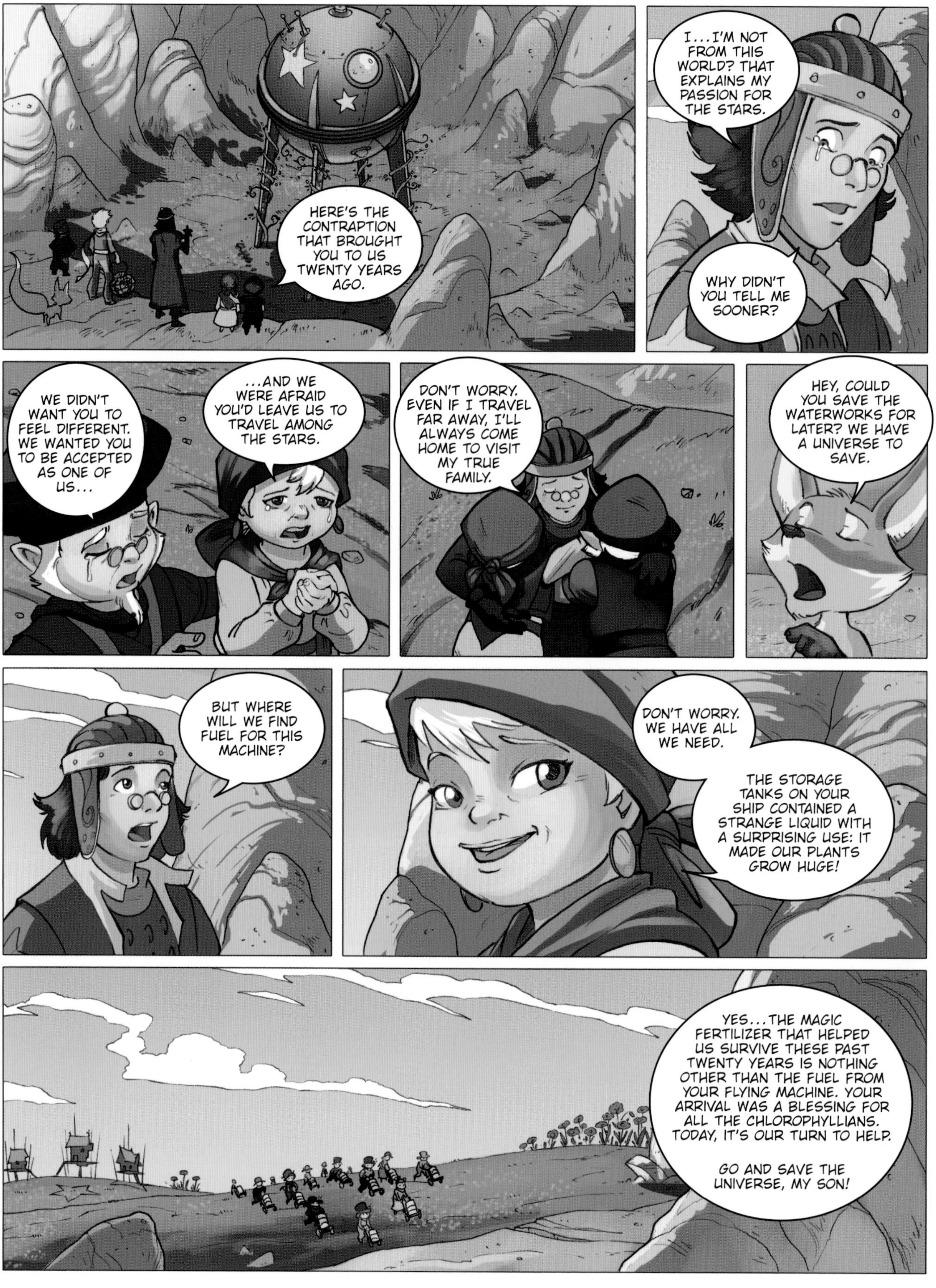
HERE'S THE CONTRAPTION THAT BROUGHT YOU TO US TWENTY YEARS AGO.
I...I'M NOT FROM THIS WORLD? THAT EXPLAINS MY PASSION FOR THE STARS.
WHY DIDN'T YOU TELL ME SOONER?
WE DIDN'T WANT YOU TO FEEL DIFFERENT. WE WANTED YOU TO BE ACCEPTED AS ONE OF US...
...AND WE WERE AFRAID YOU'D LEAVE US TO TRAVEL AMONG THE STARS.
DON'T WORRY. EVEN IF I TRAVEL FAR AWAY, I'LL ALWAYS COME HOME TO VISIT MY TRUE FAMILY.
HEY, COULD YOU SAVE THE WATERWORKS FOR LATER? WE HAVE A UNIVERSE TO SAVE.
BUT WHERE WILL WE FIND FUEL FOR THIS MACHINE?
DON'T WORRY. WE HAVE ALL WE NEED.
THE STORAGE TANKS ON YOUR SHIP CONTAINED A STRANGE LIQUID WITH A SURPRISING USE: IT MADE OUR PLANTS GROW HUGE!
YES...THE MAGIC FERTILIZER THAT HELPED US SURVIVE THESE PAST TWENTY YEARS IS NOTHING OTHER THAN THE FUEL FROM YOUR FLYING MACHINE. YOUR ARRIVAL WAS A BLESSING FOR ALL THE CHLOROPHYLLIANS. TODAY, IT'S OUR TURN TO HELP.
GO AND SAVE THE UNIVERSE, MY SON!

THIS IS FANTASTIC! ANTOINE'S SHIP IS SO FAST THAT ALL THE STARS WILL BE BACK IN THEIR PLACES IN NO TIME.

THERE, ALL DONE! WE'RE GOING BACK TO OUR PLANET. WHAT ARE YOUR PLANS, ANTOINE?

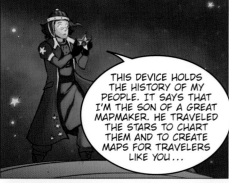

THIS DEVICE HOLDS THE HISTORY OF MY PEOPLE. IT SAYS THAT I'M THE SON OF A GREAT MAPMAKER. HE TRAVELED THE STARS TO CHART THEM AND TO CREATE MAPS FOR TRAVELERS LIKE YOU...

...BUT ONE DAY, AN INTERSTELLAR STORM FORCED HIM TO CRASH-LAND OUR SHIP ON THE PLANET OF THE CHLOROPHYLLIANS. IT'S MY DUTY TO CONTINUE HIS QUEST.

DON'T FORGET TO VISIT YOUR PARENTS FROM TIME TO TIME.

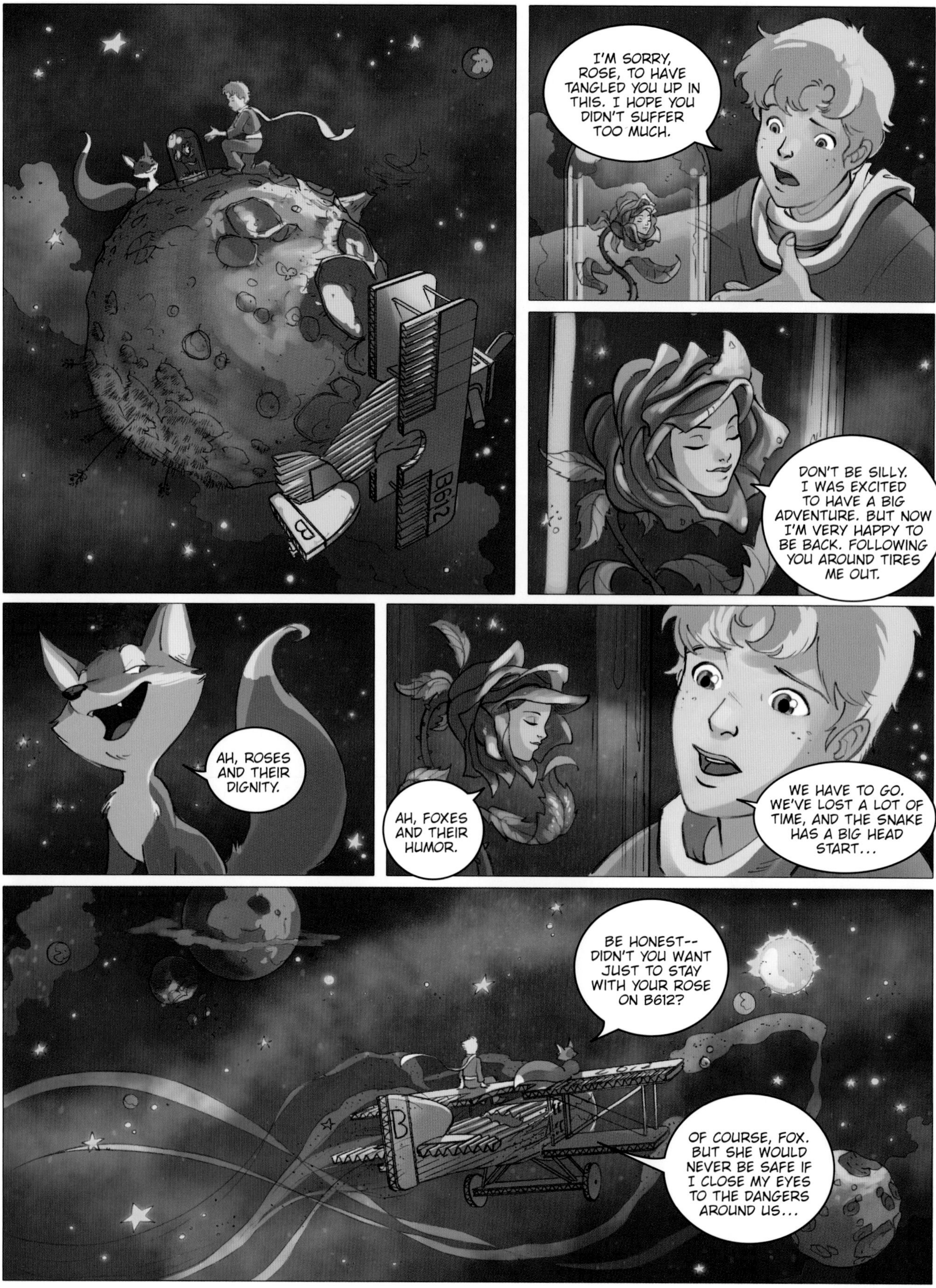

I'M SORRY, ROSE, TO HAVE TANGLED YOU UP IN THIS. I HOPE YOU DIDN'T SUFFER TOO MUCH.
DON'T BE SILLY. I WAS EXCITED TO HAVE A BIG ADVENTURE. BUT NOW I'M VERY HAPPY TO BE BACK. FOLLOWING YOU AROUND TIRES ME OUT.
AH, ROSES AND THEIR DIGNITY.
AH, FOXES AND THEIR HUMOR.
WE HAVE TO GO. WE'VE LOST A LOT OF TIME, AND THE SNAKE HAS A BIG HEAD START...
BE HONEST-- DIDN'T YOU WANT JUST TO STAY WITH YOUR ROSE ON B612?
OF COURSE, FOX. BUT SHE WOULD NEVER BE SAFE IF I CLOSE MY EYES TO THE DANGERS AROUND US...

THE END

The Little Prince

AS IMAGINED BY
PIERRE MAKYO

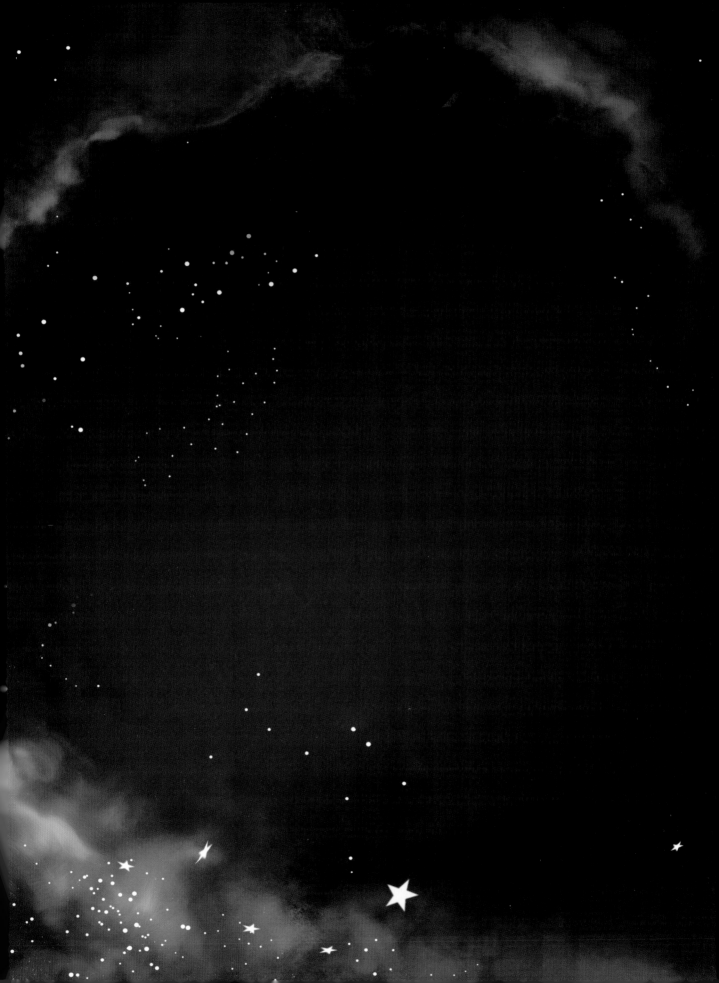

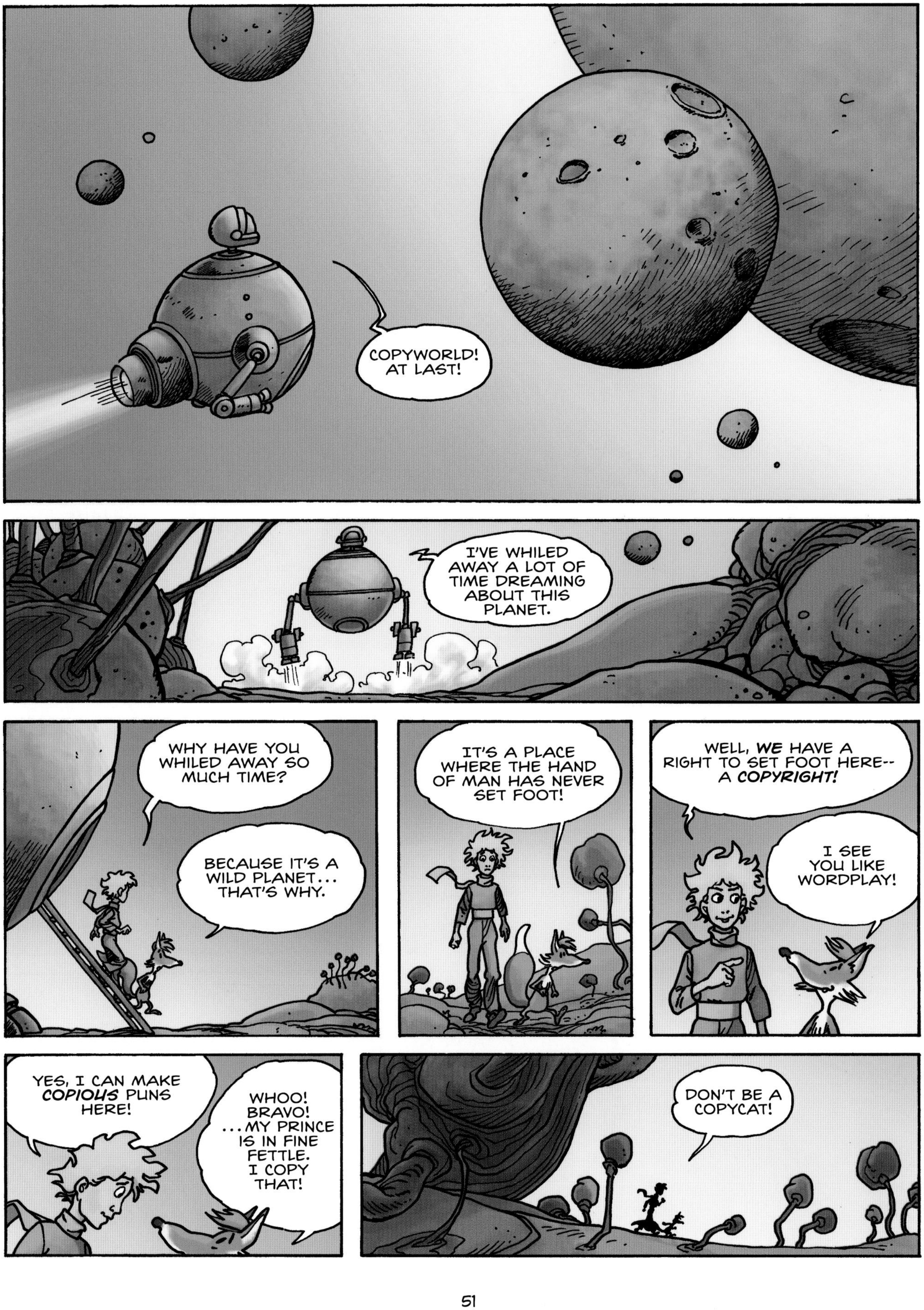
COPYWORLD! AT LAST!
I'VE WHILED AWAY A LOT OF TIME DREAMING ABOUT THIS PLANET.
WHY HAVE YOU WHILED AWAY SO MUCH TIME?
BECAUSE IT'S A WILD PLANET... THAT'S WHY.
IT'S A PLACE WHERE THE HAND OF MAN HAS NEVER SET FOOT!
WELL, WE HAVE A RIGHT TO SET FOOT HERE-- A COPYRIGHT!
I SEE YOU LIKE WORDPLAY!
YES, I CAN MAKE COPIOUS PUNS HERE!
WHOO! BRAVO! ...MY PRINCE IS IN FINE FETTLE. I COPY THAT!
DON'T BE A COPYCAT!

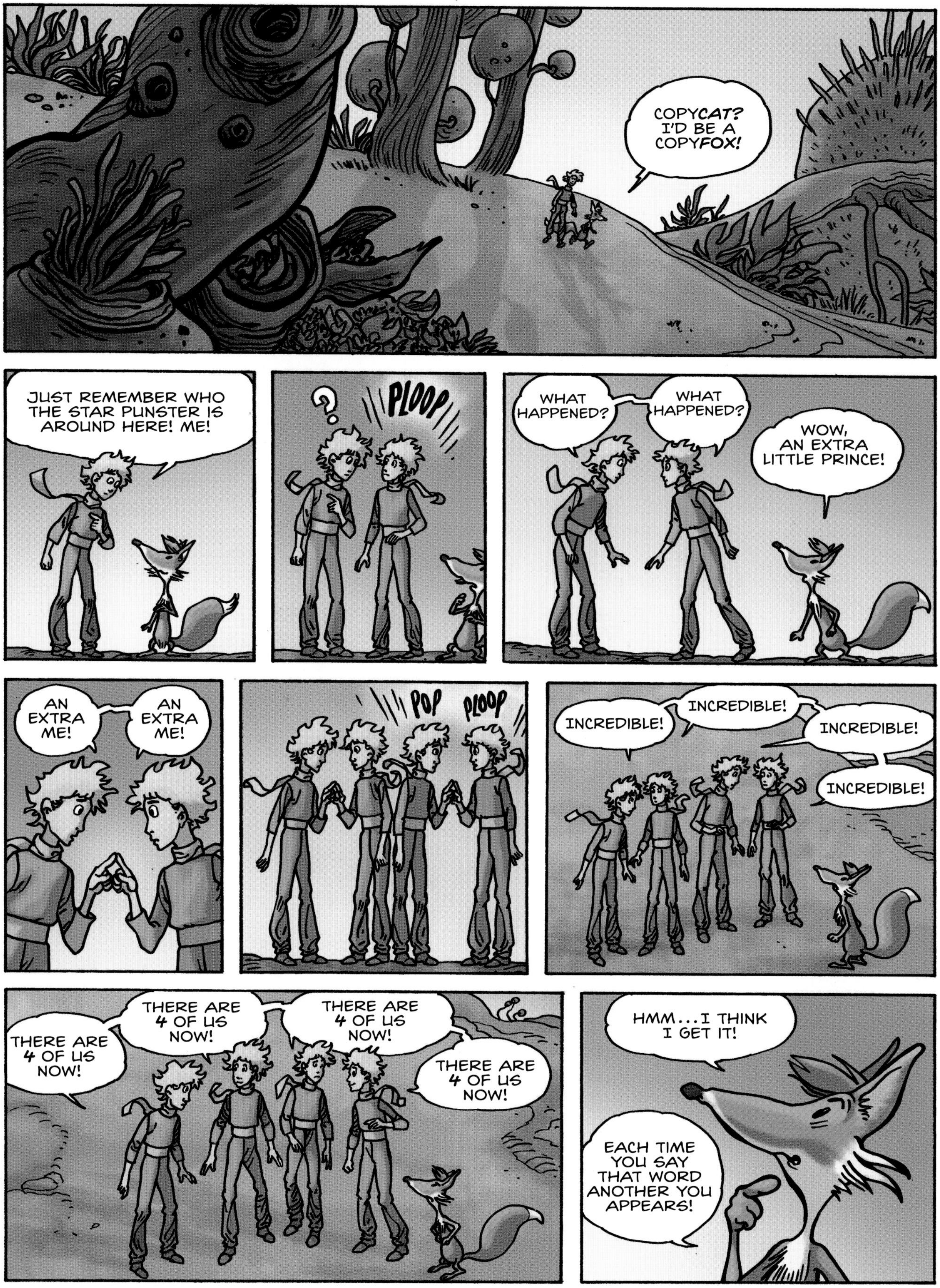
COPYCAT? I'D BE A COPYFOX!
JUST REMEMBER WHO THE STAR PUNSTER IS AROUND HERE! ME!
PLOOP
WHAT HAPPENED?
WHAT HAPPENED?
WOW, AN EXTRA LITTLE PRINCE!
AN EXTRA ME!
AN EXTRA ME!
POP
PLOOP
INCREDIBLE!
INCREDIBLE!
INCREDIBLE!
INCREDIBLE!
THERE ARE 4 OF US NOW!
THERE ARE 4 OF US NOW!
THERE ARE 4 OF US NOW!
THERE ARE 4 OF US NOW!
HMM...I THINK I GET IT!
EACH TIME YOU SAY THAT WORD ANOTHER YOU APPEARS!

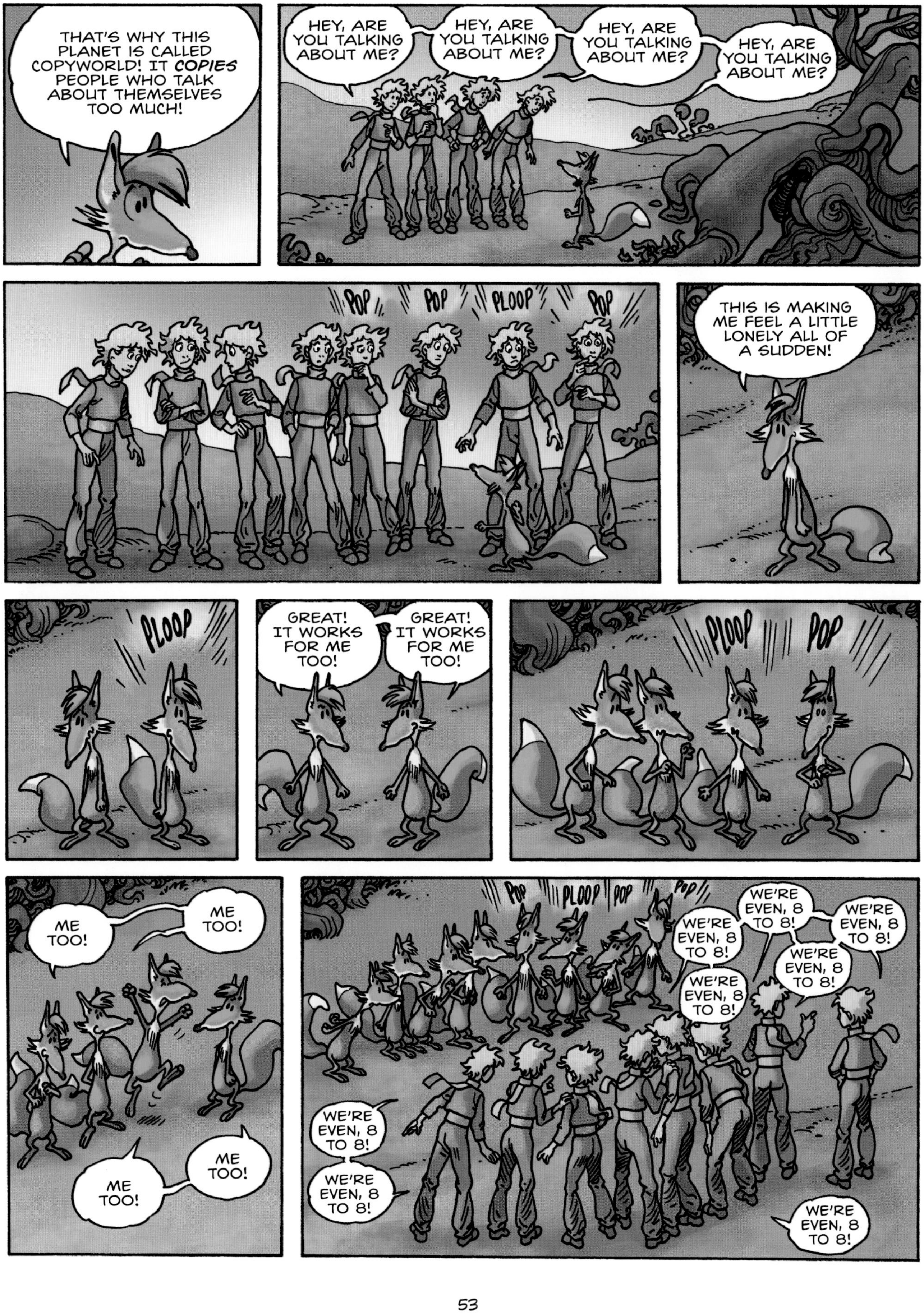
THAT'S WHY THIS PLANET IS CALLED COPYWORLD! IT COPIES PEOPLE WHO TALK ABOUT THEMSELVES TOO MUCH!
HEY, ARE YOU TALKING ABOUT ME?
HEY, ARE YOU TALKING ABOUT ME?
HEY, ARE YOU TALKING ABOUT ME?
HEY, ARE YOU TALKING ABOUT ME?
POP
POP
PLOOP
POP
THIS IS MAKING ME FEEL A LITTLE LONELY ALL OF A SUDDEN!
PLOOP
GREAT! IT WORKS FOR ME TOO!
GREAT! IT WORKS FOR ME TOO!
PLOOP
POP
ME TOO!
ME TOO!
ME TOO!
ME TOO!
POP
PLOOP
POP
POP
WE'RE EVEN, 8 TO 8!
WE'RE EVEN, 8 TO 8!
WE'RE EVEN, 8 TO 8!
WE'RE EVEN, 8 TO 8!
WE'RE EVEN, 8 TO 8!
WE'RE EVEN, 8 TO 8!
WE'RE EVEN, 8 TO 8!
WE'RE EVEN, 8 TO 8!

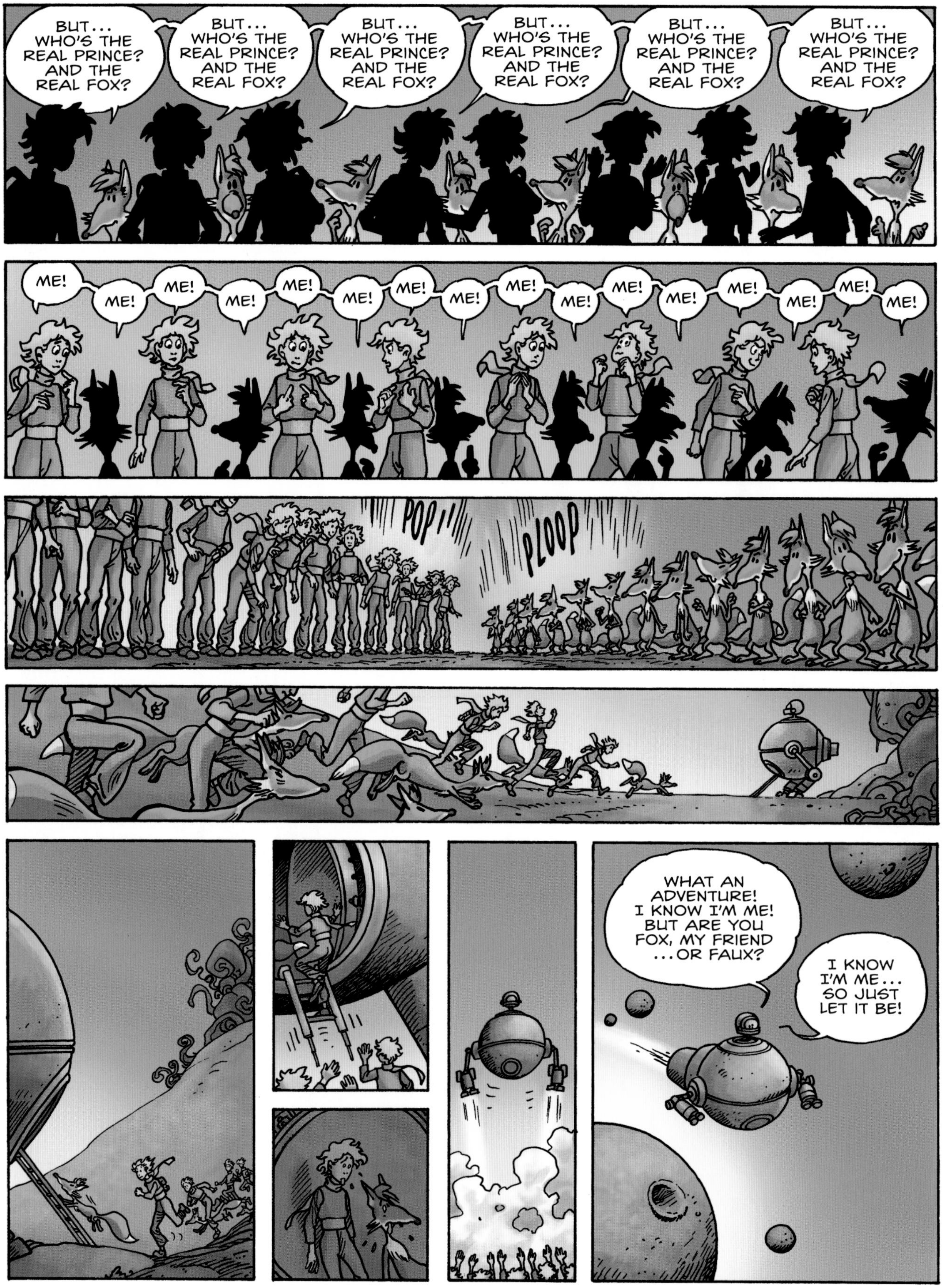
BUT... WHO'S THE REAL PRINCE? AND THE REAL FOX?
BUT... WHO'S THE REAL PRINCE? AND THE REAL FOX?
BUT... WHO'S THE REAL PRINCE? AND THE REAL FOX?
BUT... WHO'S THE REAL PRINCE? AND THE REAL FOX?
BUT... WHO'S THE REAL PRINCE? AND THE REAL FOX?
BUT... WHO'S THE REAL PRINCE? AND THE REAL FOX?
ME!
ME!
ME!
ME!
ME!
ME!
ME!
ME!
ME!
ME!
ME!
ME!
ME!
ME!
ME!
ME!
POP
PLOOP
WHAT AN ADVENTURE! I KNOW I'M ME! BUT ARE YOU FOX, MY FRIEND ...OR FAUX?
I KNOW I'M ME... SO JUST LET IT BE!

ANTOINE DE SAINT-EXUPÉRY
Aviator • Author • Adventurer • Hero

Antoine de Saint-Exupéry, author of the novel *The Little Prince* on which these new adventures are based, was born on June 29, 1900, in Lyon, France. He was the third of five children: Marie-Madeleine, Simone, Antoine, François, and Gabrielle. It was when he was twelve years old, during his summer break from boarding school, that airplanes and flying first made a huge impression on him.

In 1920, he was accepted into the École des Beaux-Arts in Paris to study architecture, but the next year he joined the Second Aviation Regiment of the armed forces and received his pilot's license. In 1922, he had his first plane crash and suffered a head fracture. He had to leave the armed forces and work at different jobs on the ground to earn a living.

By May of 1926, Saint-Exupéry was able to fly again. He delivered airmail, which was a new and sometimes dangerous profession, on routes from France to Senegal and all the way to South America. That was where, in 1931, he met and married Consuelo Suncin.

From 1933 to 1938, Saint-Exupéry was very busy. He traveled to North Africa and Indochina and attempted to break the flight speed record from Paris to Saigon, Vietnam—during which his plane crashed again. It went down in the middle of the Sahara Desert. After his recovery, his life became even busier. He wrote newspaper reports in Spain on the Spanish Civil War, scouted airplane routes between Casablanca and Timbuktu, wrote a screenplay, registered several patents, and traveled to the United States. In 1939, with the start of World War II, he returned to France and talked his way into a job as a high-risk reconnaissance pilot for the French Air Force. But this only lasted until France reached an armistice agreement with Germany.

In December 1940, Saint-Exupéry returned to visit friends in New York, where he finally began work on *The Little Prince.* The story is narrated by a pilot who has crashed his plane into the Sahara Desert. He meets a little prince visiting from a faraway asteroid. Along the way, the prince also meets Fox and Snake. By late 1942, after spending the spring and summer writing and illustrating, Saint-Exupéry had completed his novel, and in April 1943 it was published in his native language of French *(Le Petit Prince)* and in English.

Saint-Exupéry was eager to return to the war. He decided to join the Free French Forces in Algeria, who were continuing the fight against the Axis powers. Because of his age, at first he had a hard time convincing them to let him fly. He was authorized to fly five dangerous missions. In fact, he flew eight. On July 31, 1944, Saint-Exupéry went on a scouting flight to prepare for military landings in the south of France. His plane disappeared over the water, and he was never seen again.

Over the decades since *The Little Prince* was published, it has gone on to become one of the best-selling novels of all time. In 2003, a small moon in our solar system's asteroid belt was named Petit-Prince in honor of the masterpiece Saint-Exupéry created.

THE LITTLE PRINCE IN THE TWENTY-FIRST CENTURY

The Little Prince is a landmark of literature and one of the most translated and beloved books in the world. It tackles universal topics with a unique philosophical and poetic sensibility. Sixty-five years after the first edition, the Saint-Exupéry Estate decided to bring the character back for a whole new generation . . . and for everyone who has ever loved the boy who sees the world with his heart.

The Little Prince now returns in a series of new adventures that remain true to the spirit of the original work. He will travel from planet to planet chasing the wicked Snake, who wants to plunge the whole universe into darkness. On each planet, the Snake sends bad thoughts into the minds of its inhabitants, making them sad and grim, draining the life out of their planet. The Little Prince must leave his beautiful Rose behind and must use his vision and courage to defeat the Snake, bringing along his friend Fox to save planets in danger across the universe.

ABOUT THE ADAPTERS

After several years in video games and Japanese animation, adapter Guillaume Dorison became literary editor for the publisher Les Humanoïdes Associés in 2006, where he launched the Shogun Collection dedicated to original manga. In June 2010, he founded Élyum Studio with Didier Poli, Jean-Baptiste Hostache, and Xavier Dorison to provide services for the creation of graphic novels. In addition to his position as director of writing for Élyum Studio, he has more than two dozen comics and manga to his credit under the pseudonym IZU, has written several titles in the Explora series on world explorers for French publisher Glénat, and won the 2010 Animeland Prize for best French manga.

Didier Poli, artistic director for the new graphic novel adaptations based on *The Little Prince*, was born in Lyon in 1971. After graduate studies in applied arts, he worked for various animation studios including Disney. He was working as artistic director for the video game company Kalisto Entertainment when he met Manuel Bichebois in 2001 and began drawing Bichebois's graphic novel series L'Enfant de l'orage. At the 2004 Nîmes Festival, Didier Poli received the Bronze Boar prize for young talent. He continues, along with his work on graphic novels, to work regularly in cartoons and video games as a designer and storyboard artist.

The Little Prince
BOOK 1: THE PLANET OF WIND

The Little Prince
BOOK 2: THE PLANET OF THE FIREBIRD

The Little Prince
BOOK 3: THE PLANET OF MUSIC

The Little Prince
BOOK 4: THE PLANET OF JADE

The Little Prince
BOOK 5: THE STAR SNATCHER'S PLANET

The Little Prince
BOOK 6: THE PLANET OF THE NIGHT GLOBES

The Little Prince
BOOK 7: THE PLANET OF THE OVERHEARERS

The Little Prince
BOOK 8: THE PLANET OF THE TORTOISE DRIVER

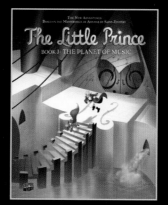

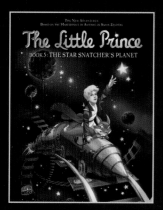

Book 1: The Planet of Wind

Book 2: The Planet of the Firebird

Book 3: The Planet of Music

Book 4: The Planet of Jade

Book 5: The Star Snatcher's Planet

Book 6: The Planet of the Night Globes

Book 7: The Planet of the Overhearers

Book 8: The Planet of the Tortoise Driver

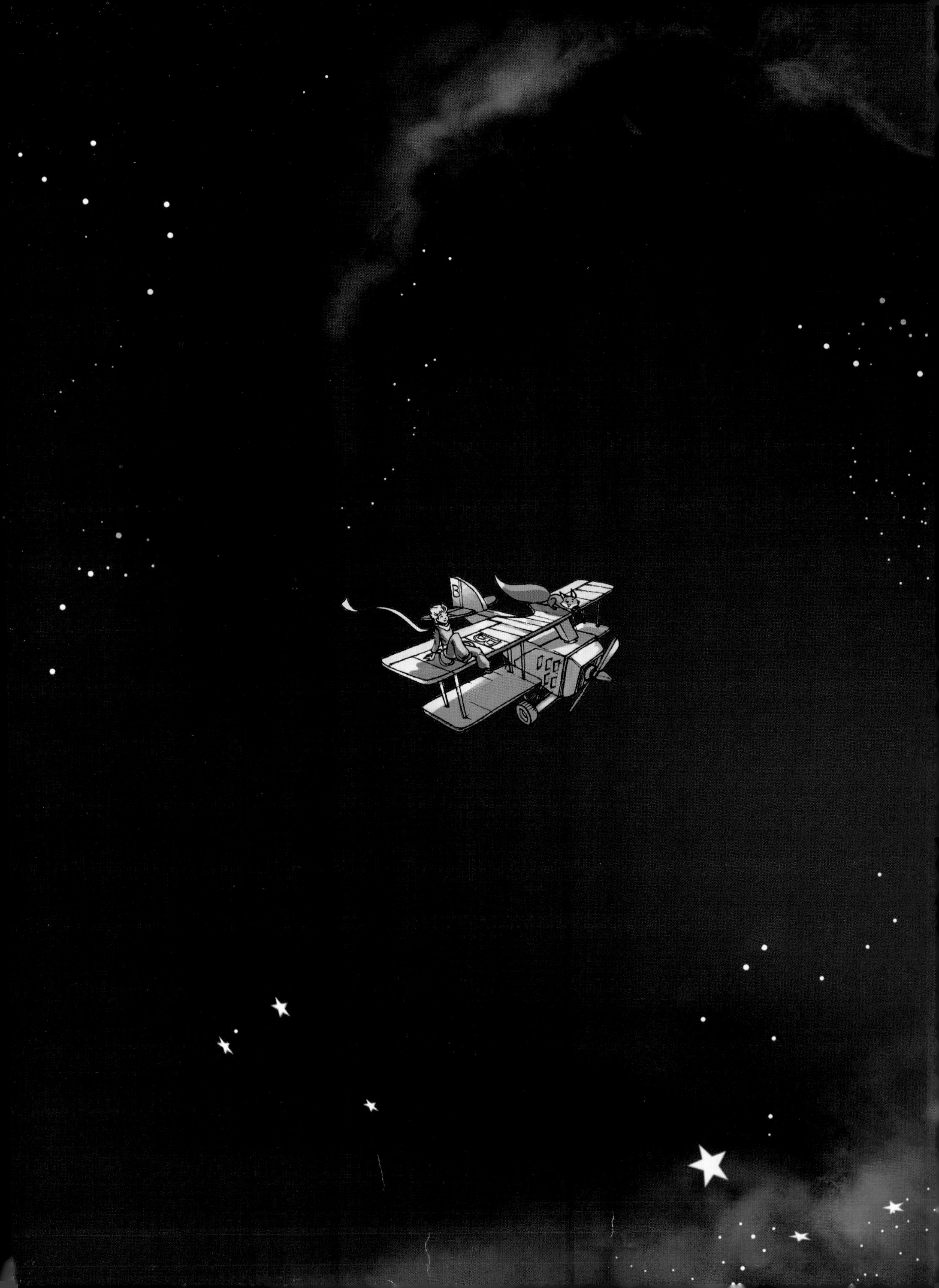